RED DIRT HEART

N.R. WALKER

COPYRIGHT

INFORMATION PRIOR TO READING AND GLOSSARY

Size matters

Sutton Station, while fictional, is based on a working property in the middle of Australia and is three hours drive to the nearest town. Sutton Station is 2.58 million acres (10,441 square kilometres). To compare, the largest ranch in the USA is King Ranch at 825,000 acres (3340 square kilometres).

Sutton station is the third biggest station in the Northern Territory and is classed as desert. Sutton Station is approximately the same size as Lebanon.

The Northern Territory is a federal territory in between Queensland and Western Australia. It's like state, just don't call it that to someone who lives there.

Australian Terminology Glossary:

Station: Farm, ranch.

Paddock: Large fenced area for cattle; a
    pasture.
Holding yard: Corral.
Swag: A canvas bedroll.
Ute: Utility pick-up truck.
Motorbike: Motorcycle, dirtbike.
Akubra: Australian cowboy hat.
Scone: American sweet biscuit, usually
    eaten with cream and jam.

N.R. WALKER

Red
DIRT
HEART

CHAPTER ONE

WHERE THE AMERICAN GUY WALKS IN, ALL
BLUE EYES AND DISARMING SMILES, AND MY
LIFE GOES TO SHIT.

JUST ON SUNDOWN, I got off the motorbike, kicked the stand down so the bike stood upright without me and closed the gate. I'd been out all day in the South paddocks doing a final check of fences and water trough pumps before we brought the cattle down from the North. I'd seen the ute back at the homestead as I came in so I knew George was home.

George was my leading hand. He was in his fifties, with greying hair and sun-hardened skin. He'd worked here for as long I could remember, but he was more than a loyal employee. He was my friend, and in a lot of ways, more of a dad to me than my own old man ever was.

He'd been out all day, left before sun-up and headed into Alice Springs. We were a good three hours from the nearest town, and with a list as long as his arm from the Station cook, Ma—who also happened to be his wife—he needed a few hours in town before heading out to the airport to pick up the real reason for his trip: an American agronomy student by the name of Travis Craig.

When my father ran this farm, or station as we called

it, every year we'd have people from another country come and spend a couple of weeks as part of some Diversification exchange program. My old man always said it was a good way to source out what other countries were teaching, but really I think he just liked the extra pair of hands at the finish of the dry season. And when we'd had a phone call back in July to ask if we'd be interested in hosting another student, and given it'd been a few years, I thought it seemed like a good idea. Now I couldn't help but wonder if this Travis Craig would be a help or a liability.

I rode the bike into the yard and pulled up in the shed. I figured they'd know I'd arrived, having heard the bike, so I headed straight for the house. Like most homesteads built almost a hundred years ago, it was a weatherboard home, with an old iron roof and a veranda around four sides to try and keep it cool.

I kicked the red dust from my boots on the veranda steps and tried to brush the same from my jeans, took off my hat before I opened the door and walked inside. There was a suitcase and a duffel bag near the front door and voices at the back of the house.

"In the kitchen," George called out.

I followed the sound of chatter and the smell of something good to find a meeting of sorts in the old country-style kitchen. The worn, solid wooden table that graced the middle of the room was covered with plates of scones and trays of cups and tea, and three people were in chairs around it—my right-hand man, George, his wife the cook, Ma, and a stranger with short light-brown hair and pale blue eyes.

George was the first to his feet, and the man beside him soon followed. "Here's the boss, Charles Sutton," George said, introducing me formally. "Charlie, this is Travis Craig."

Travis looked about twenty-two years old, not much younger than me. Whereas I was a stockier build, with dull brown hair and boring brown eyes, he was taller than me by a few inches and muscular and lean. He held out his hand and smiled. "Mr Sutton. It's a pleasure to meet you." His accent was strange to hear at first, but his smile was warm and wide.

I wiped my hand on my shirt and held it out for him to shake. "Travis," I said with a nod. "Please, call me Charlie."

He seemed nervous or uncertain, so I figured I'd take the emphasis off him. I threw my dusty old hat onto the table and sat down across from our guest. "Jeez, Ma," I said, looking at the food on the table. "How many are you feeding?"

"I made 'em for you. They're your favourite," she said.

"Are they *pumpkin* scones?" I asked.

"'Course," she said proudly. "You boys can finish them for dessert."

I reached out to grab one, and Ma's hand came out to stop me. "Not with those dirty hands, Mister. And you can get your hat off my table."

George chuckled at me, and I looked at Travis and grinned. "I can't win."

Ma stood up. "Go and show Travis which room is his, then you can clean yourself up for dinner," she said to me. She glanced at the clock on the kitchen wall. "Forty minutes, boys."

I pushed my chair out from the table, and taking his cue, Travis did the same. I got to the door and seeing Ma had her back turned, I quickly grabbed a buttered scone off the table.

"Charles Sutton!" Ma cried, catching me red-handed.

I smiled as I shoved the scone in my mouth, but I was quick to duck around the door, out of the flight path of any kitchen utensils Ma might launch at me. Normally she just threatened me with a ladle or tea towel, but over the years—especially when I was a teenager—if I came in and started picking while she was cooking, I'd have to duck the odd cooking implement.

I laughed down the hallway, and Travis was just a step behind me. He smiled right back at me, and I had to chew and swallow my mouthful of food before I could speak. "I'll show you to your room," I told him. I put my hat on the middle hook, as always, picked up his suitcase and left the duffel bag for him. "You'll stay in the main house while you're here. There's three worker's cottages, but they're taken. You'll meet the other guys at dinner."

I led him through a door off the foyer to a door halfway down the hall. "Your room," I said, walking in and putting his suitcase on the queen-size bed. There was a dresser and a wardrobe, and the window was open, but the curtain was still. "Your room faces east. You'll get the early morning sun, not the heat of the afternoon."

"It's a beautiful house," Travis said. His accent was softened along with his tone.

"Thank you," I said with smile. It *is* a beautiful house. The homestead itself was built in the nineteen twenties, had wooden floors and nine-foot ceilings. "It's old and takes a lot of upkeep these days, but she's been well looked after."

"They don't make big old houses like these anymore," he said. "Even back home, old traditional ranch houses are few and far between."

"Where exactly is *back home*?" I asked. "Texas, yeah?"

Travis put his duffel bag on the bed. "Yes, sir. Johnson City is just west of Austin. My family has a ranch there."

"Cattle, yes?"

"Yes, sir. Brahman."

"Please don't call me sir."

"Sorry. It's a habit my momma drilled into me."

"It's okay," I said reassuringly. "I just look for my father when I hear that word."

Travis nodded but looked down to his luggage on the bed. He was a few inches taller than my five foot ten, and a fairly decent build, wore a checkered shirt with sleeves rolled to his elbows, American jeans and fancy cowboy boots. But what I noticed most was when he looked downward like that I could see the outline of the back of his neck. It was tanned, muscular with short, clipped hair that looked as though it'd be real soft to touch...

"I'm sorry," he said, snapping me out my wayward thoughts. "I guess I was expecting the boss to be a lot older..."

I studied him for a long moment. "Is that a problem?"

His head shot up and his eyes were wide. "Oh no, not at all," he said quickly. "It's just my father mentioned a man named Charles was about his age, not mine..."

"Charles was my father," I told him. "And his father before that and probably the one before that."

He nodded and looked back down to his belongings on the bed. "Mine is a family name too."

He was obviously a little uncomfortable with my being there, so I figured I'd leave him be and let him settle in. I walked to the door and said, "I'll leave you to it. Bathroom is the door at the end of the hall to your left. My room's the first door near the foyer on your right." I wasn't exactly sure why I said that, so I added, "If you need anything, that is.

And George and Ma live in this house too, in the bedroom off the back sunroom, but they're quiet as mice. You won't hear a peep from them until breakfast time."

Travis smiled at me then. "Thanks."

"I guess I should tell you the rules of the house," I said, figuring it was probably best to get all the formalities out of the way.

"Rules?"

"Yep, rules. Breakfast is at six on the dot. If we're in and around the yard, lunch is twelve noon. If we're out during the day, Ma will usually pack us some lunch or drive something out to us or we'll pack it and take it with us. Dinner is six sharp—" I looked at my watch. "—which is in twenty minutes, so I'd better let you freshen up. Oh, and just a reminder that Sutton Station is dry; there is no alcohol here. The crew of workers usually head to the Alice every second weekend to let loose, but there's no drinking here."

"The Alice?"

"Alice Springs," I explained. "Locals call it *the* Alice. Dunno why."

Travis nodded again, almost smiling. "Okay."

"And the boys'll probably wanna give you a hard time, you know, as the greenhorn, but they won't mean anything by it," I said with a smile. "They're a good bunch. But you'll be with me to start off with so they won't be game to try nothing."

"Thanks," he said with half a smile.

"Like I said, you'll meet them at dinner," I told him. "We eat in the main house. Most big stations will have different quarters for workers to eat, but there's only six full-time staff...well," I corrected, "seven including you, so we just use this house. And they're all scared of Ma. She has rules at the table and they respect them."

"More rules?"

I grinned at him. "Be on time, be clean, be grateful. Wear a shirt and shoes, and *never* wear your hat at the table."

Travis chuckled, a deep throaty sound. "Sounds just like my momma."

I found myself smiling back at him. "Could she throw a rolling pin at your head?"

"From about thirty yards," Travis said with a grin. "But when you make it out of the kitchen without bein' caught, you know the worst part?"

We both spoke at the same time. "You gotta come home sometime."

We both laughed, and he seemed a lot more comfortable when I left him to unpack. I cleaned up first, washed my hands and face and even brushed my hair, then went back to the kitchen. I kissed Ma on the cheek so she'd forgive me for stealing a scone earlier and grabbed a bottle of water from the fridge.

"He seems like a real nice fella," Ma said.

"He does."

"Think he'll last?"

I shrugged. "He's from a farm back home, so who knows..." I took a mouthful of water. "I hope he does."

Ma smiled into the pot on the stove. "He's kinda cute."

"Ma," I warned. "Please don't."

"Just stating a fact, sweetheart," she said. Then she held out her hand. "Pass me the pepper."

And the conversation on how *cute* Travis was, was thankfully over. I had to work with the man for the next four weeks. He was a guest in my house, and I was responsible for his welfare. The last thing I needed was to start thinking of him in *that* way.

Ten minutes later, he walked into the kitchen, show-ered, looking all bright-eyed and fresh, dressed in jeans and a tee-shirt, smelling all clean and of a deodorant I didn't recognise. I turned back to the sink, trying to ignore thoughts that weren't rightfully pure.

Fuck.

Ma hummed, "Hmm mm," so only I could hear, in a *that's-what-I-thought* kind of way. I tried to leave, but she stopped me. "Set the table for me, boys."

I sighed, knowing it was futile to argue with Ma in her kitchen. I opened the door to the dry storage pantry and gave a nod to Travis for him to join me. I put the sauces and condiments on a tray and handed it to him to hold and then raided the fridge for mustards. I grabbed the cutlery, and Travis followed me into the dining room where we got the table ready for dinner.

"Everything okay?" I asked him.

"Oh sure, it's just..." He shook his head. "Never mind."

"Say it. I'm not easily offended."

He smiled and exhaled loudly. "It's just that you're the boss, right?"

"Yes."

He looked back toward the kitchen door, and spoke softly. "But Ma gives you orders...and she full-named you... When my momma calls me by my full name..." He shook his head. "I know it ain't ever good."

I laughed at that. "The kitchen is a room where anyone can speak freely. Plus, Ma is the boss of the kitchen; it's her domain. But it's where we don't talk business, we talk...like a family." I shrugged. "Ma and George as good as raised me."

"Oh."

I smiled, not wanting to sully the mood. "Out of the

kitchen, it's a different story. Don't know why, it's just the way it's always been."

He opened his mouth to say something but stopped when George walked into the room. "Dinner smells good. We should have overseas visitors every day."

"Dinner's always good. You'll do well to remember that," Ma said behind him and put two dishes of roasted veggies in the middle of the table.

George smiled as he sat down. "Need help, dear?"

She rolled her eyes as she walked out, only to return with dishes of greens and gravy. I sat at the head of the table, with George on my right and indicated to Travis that he should sit on my other side. "Take a seat."

"Shouldn't I help Ma bring something in?"

George snorted. "Only if you have a death wish, son."

"I heard that, Joseph Brown," Ma said, giving her husband a death stare. She put the tray of sliced roast beef in the centre of the table. "I don't help you boys do your job, you don't help me do mine."

I smiled at her, and she winked at me. When she'd gone, Travis looked at me and George, apparently confused. "Joseph Brown?"

"That's my real name," George said. "But I've been the foreman here for twenty years, so they called me George, as in George Foreman."

"Right," Travis said with a smile. "Of course."

Just then, we heard the back door open and the sound of voices and feet on the floorboards, and then the six other station hands walked in. I thought Travis might be a little intimidated, but to my surprise, he stood up.

"Guys," I said, "this is Travis Craig, the fella from America. Travis, this is Fish, Trudy, Bacon, Mick, Ernie and Billy."

Travis walked from his seat at the table to shake their hands. They introduced themselves again individually, smiling, but still sizing the poor guy up. He did well to hold his own. For everyone's benefit, I added, "Travis, if you've got any questions and either me or George aren't here, you go find Billy. He's my leading stockman, ain't that right, Billy?"

"Too right, boss," he said.

Billy was an Indigenous man: dark skin, black wiry hair and a smile that took up half his face. He was also a bloody good stockman who knew his way around cattle and he understood the nature of this land. He'd worked here for about seven years, and I'd be lost without him.

When everyone was seated, the questions started, aimed at the American man seated to my left.

"You can ride a horse?"

"Yes."

"A motorbike?"

"A motorcycle? Yes."

"How old are ya?"

"Twenty-three."

"Live on a farm?"

"Yes. Near Austin, Texas."

"Well, you're already better than the last guy," Mick said with a snort. "Poor guy from...where was he from?"

"England," I answered.

"Poor kid," George said. "The sun near cooked him. That was a few years ago now though."

"Couldn't ride a horse when he got here," Fish said. "Funniest thing I ever saw."

"What was he doing here?" Travis asked. "If he didn't have a clue?"

"It was a student placement thing," I said. "He was

studying agricultural science and wanted to know how farmers lived in the desert, apparently." Then I added, "I wasn't here."

Ma walked into the room then, carrying a basket of freshly baked rolls. It was always the last thing she put on the table before everyone dug into their grub.

"Thanks, Ma," everyone said in unison.

"Looks real good, Mrs Ma," Billy said. He gave her one of his disarming grins and she patted his shoulder.

"Okay" was all she said, and it was cue for everyone at the table to eat.

I must admit, Ma's general rule of manners at her table was a godsend. Yes, these people earned their dinner. They worked hard, and they sure worked up an appetite, and I'd be certain to think if Ma wasn't there to keep 'em in line, they'd eat with their hands.

But civility—as much as the Outback allowed—prevailed. They ate with cutlery, asked politely for plates to be passed down, for someone to pass the butter, and there were even pleases and thank yous.

We were quiet as we ate and when everyone had had his or her fill, the conversation slowly started. Travis answered politely if asked something, but for the most part just watched and listened as everyone was getting excited about the coming final muster of the year and the promise of the wet season.

Rain.

It meant busy times for me and my workers, but we'd had a good season, and I had a real good team. I demanded 110% and they gave it. As reward, they got looked after. That's how things out here worked.

After Ma had served the afternoon-made scones with jam and cream—which were quickly devoured—they left and the house was quiet. I went into the office, while George took Travis out to the front veranda to watch the sun finally call it a day.

As I caught up on some paperwork, I could hear parts of their muted conversation. Not that I was listening on purpose, but they were sitting near my window.

"It's really very beautiful," Travis said. His accent was intriguing. "Not sure I've ever seen a sky that colour orange."

"Yes, it is beautiful," George answered. After a short silence, he asked, "How you findin' it so far?"

"Everyone's great," Travis answered quickly. "I will admit, I was expecting Charlie to be older. I didn't think the boss of a place like this would be about my age."

My ears pricked up at the mention of my name, and I put the papers in my hand on the desk and listened.

"He's a real good man," George said. "I worked for his dad before him and will work for Charlie for as long as he'll have me. He's a tough boss. He doesn't take shit from no one and he expects a lot, but he's fair. When he first took over, a lot of men wouldn't work for him. Nothing against Charlie, in fact, just the opposite; they thought he was too tough. It just meant the men who had the balls to stay were the best."

I smiled at that, but I tuned them out and concentrated on emails, invoices and the mail. It was my least favourite part of my job, and a few hours every night after dinner I would try and keep on top of the paperwork side of the station.

It was getting kinda late when I shut the laptop down and headed to bed. As I walked into the foyer on the way to my room, I noticed the front door was still open. I stuck my head outside to see if I wasn't about to turn the lights out on anyone when I saw Travis sitting by himself on one of the seats on the front veranda.

I opened the door slowly, wondering if something was wrong. "Everything alright?"

He looked over at me and smiled. "Yeah, sure," he said. "It's just so nice out here." I sat down next to him, and he was quick to add, "I'm not keeping you up, am I?"

"Nah," I said, leaning back in the chair, and I let out a sigh. "It is nice out here this time of night."

"It's incredibly quiet."

"You jet-lagged or something?" I asked.

"No, no," he said. "I had four days in Sydney before I flew out here. I slept the first day."

I nodded, not sure what to say. I never was very good at making conversation.

"You've got a good team," he said. "They seem like a good group of people."

"They are. They might try and see if you're worth your salt, but they mean no harm."

"Can I ask you something?"

I looked out into the darkness, not sure if I'd like his question. "Sure."

"What's with the nicknames?" he asked. "Everyone's got a weird name."

I laughed. "Dunno. Just what Aussies do. If we can't shorten a surname, we'll shorten it anyway. Like Fish is short for Fisher. But Ernie's real name is Chris. I dunno where in the name the *Ernie* part comes from."

"And Bacon?"

"Well, he comes from a pig farm..."

He threw his head back and laughed. It was a deep rumbling sound that made it impossible to not smile. Impossible not to look at him. "And Trudy's the only woman?"

"She is," I said with a nod. "But don't be fooled. She's the toughest of the lot and has a helluva right hook."

Travis's eyes went wide. "She punched you?"

"Not me. But I've heard about it. In town once, some guy was thinkin' he could say something to her that was outta line, and well"—I shook my head—"they really shouldn't do that."

He laughed. "I'll keep that in mind."

"So tell me," I said, changing topic. "A degree in Agronomy?"

"Agricultural science, yes," he said. "Soil properties, climate, production, that kind of thing."

"If you've studied the ecoregions of Texas, what made you want to come here?" I asked. "I mean, we have different soil types, different climates, different crops, weather patterns, production systems. I've never been to Texas," I admitted, "but I'd imagine the human dimensions of inter-action with the land here are far removed from what you've studied."

Travis looked at me, like really stared. A slow smile spread across his face. "You sound like you know what you're talking about."

I scoffed. "Don't sound so surprised. I'm not *just* a red-dirt junkie."

"You studied agricultural sciences?"

"I did," I answered. "I didn't graduate though. I had to come back here to run this place."

"How far'd you get?"

"Did three years out of four."

He made a face. "Oh, man. That sucks," he said softly, but then he looked back out into the darkness as though he understood something about responsibilities. "I graduated," he said. "And you talk about differences in soil diversity and productions like it doesn't make sense for me to come here where it is so different from what I studied. But that's *why* I came here. Because it's different."

Then he started talking about learning how to think outside of what he knew. He claimed he already knew about farming Texas land, and the science behind it was academic. What good was learning what he already knew, he said. But he couldn't learn in any book how we farmed the desert out here. What he really wanted to learn, he said, was how to achieve the same goals using different rules.

I asked him why he'd need it. "If you're only going to farm Texan land, what difference does it make how we do it out here?"

"I know how to achieve maximum yield back home, theoretically," he said. "But if I can see how someone else might achieve the same while faced with different circumstances, it has to be beneficial to how a ranch is run." He was quiet for a while, like his words had run out of steam. "I guess I'm just trying to be lateral in my thinking."

I smiled at him. "Well, I hope to learn as much from you as you from me."

He leaned back in his chair and lifted his wrist to his face. "Shoot! Look at the time!"

I checked my watch. It was almost one in the morning. Jesus, we'd been talking for hours.

Travis stood up. "Sorry to have kept you up."

I stood up too. "Don't apologise. Not your fault."

"What time do we get up?" he asked.

"Five. I usually do a bit before breakfast."

He nodded. "And I shouldn't be late, yeah?"

I smiled and held the front door open for him. "No, you're working with the boss tomorrow, and he's a cranky bastard."

Travis smiled, knowing I was talking about myself, and walked inside. "Goodnight."

I turned the veranda light off, walked into my room, stripped down to my undies and climbed into bed. I found myself smiling as I lay there, thinking of Travis—of someone who I could *talk* to—and told myself not to see what wasn't there. Despite my thoughts, I was quick to sleep and dreamed of a man with a Texan drawl and eyes the colour of the morning sky.

CHAPTER TWO

I WAS up before the sun, just like always, despite the lack of sleep. I was in the kitchen getting under Ma's feet, just like always, when Travis stood at the door. He was dressed and ready for the day, even if he still looked a little sleepy. I gave him a nod good morning and suddenly found what Ma what doing very interesting in hopes that Travis couldn't somehow tell I'd dreamed of him.

"Get the boy a cup of tea," Ma ordered me.

I looked at Travis then and had to clear my throat so I could speak. "I think he might prefer coffee…"

Ma spun to look at him. "You don't like my tea?"

"Um, it's not that I don't like *your* tea…well, I…" He looked at me for help.

I snorted out a laugh. "Americans don't drink hot tea like we do, Ma. They drink it cold."

"Cold?" Ma said. "Why the hell didn't you say something, boy?"

"Um," Travis said hesitatingly. "I didn't want to offend anyone."

Ma stared at me. "Well, what are you waiting for? Make the man some coffee."

I quickly spooned a teaspoon of instant coffee into a cup and added boiling water from the kettle. "Milk or sugar?" I asked him.

"Both."

Right. *Why the fuck was I nervous?* I put the coffee cup down on the table and took a spoon off the serving tray, but before I opened the sugar bowl, Ma clucked her tongue at me. "Just take the whole tray out," she said with a sigh. "Get out of my kitchen, please, love. The boys'll be in any minute and you're in the road."

Travis pressed his lips together like he was trying not to smile, and I rolled my eyes. "Here," I said, handing him his cup. I carried the tray into the dining room, and he followed me in. Putting the tray on the sideboard, I sat the milk jug and sugar bowl on the table near his seat.

His seat.

Jesus. He hadn't even been here a day, and I'd already given him a seat at the table.

The seat right next to mine.

"Been up long?" he asked, obviously trying to make small talk because I was lost in my head overthinking shit again.

"Yeah," I said, standing at the sideboard, making myself a cup of tea, figuring it would calm me a bit. "I'm always up with the sparrows. I let the dogs off and feed 'em some breakfast. People tell me I spoil 'em, but I don't. I just look after 'em."

"What kind of dogs?"

"Kelpies. I've got four of 'em. They do the work of ten men in the paddock so of course I look after them." I sat down in my seat, next to Travis, and sipped my tea. "You sleep okay for your first night?"

"I did, thank you," he said, then sipped his coffee and made a face.

I laughed. "I'll tell Ma to add nicer coffee on the list?"

He nodded but laughed quietly. "Or I could just drink swamp water."

George walked in and went straight for the sideboard for a cuppa. I thought he might have something to say about me smiling before breakfast, but he thankfully kept it to himself. The other guys soon filed in, followed by Ma and dishes of eggs, bacon, snags, fried tomato and toast.

We talked about what needed doing while we cleaned up everything Ma served us, the dining room cleared out as soon as it filled, and we all got on with our day. I picked my hat off the rack in the hall on my way out and put it on. Travis was staring at the top of my head. I grinned at him. "What?"

"What the hell happened to your hat?"

I pulled the old Akubra off my head and looked at it. Travis, on the other hand, poked it with his finger. "Hey," I said. "Don't knock my hat."

He was still staring at it. "How does it keep in shape? Not that it does very well."

"Well, it's old... I wear it every day." I turned the hat over, looking at it from all angles. The felt was now dirty, stained and had holes across the brim and crown. It was barely holding together. "Plus it's been stomped on, stood on by man, bull and horse, pulled out of a river, ridden over, lost, found... I dropped it out of the helicopter once." I looked at his hat. "Actually, that cap you're wearing is no good for the sun out here."

I looked at the hat rack. There were three hooks on a

strip of painted timber, head-height in the hall near the front door. The hook on the left was where George kept his hat, mine was the middle hook, and the hook on the right, closest to the door, had sat bare since my father died.

"I'll get you a better hat," I said, disappearing into my room. I pulled my old-*old* hat from the back of my wardrobe and took it out to him. "This is my old one. It's a bit worn," I said, dusting it off.

"It's in better condition than yours," Travis said, eyeing it dubiously.

"Yeah, but this one"—I pulled on the brim of my hat—"is my favourite." I handed him the old hat. "See if it fits."

He took off his cap and tried the old Akubra on. It fit him okay. He pulled on the crown of it, shufflin' it 'til it felt right. "Better?"

I gave him a nod. "Much."

He looked again at my hat and shook his head. Then his eyes narrowed. "You dropped it out of a helicopter?"

"Yep. Use one for mustering and I must have leaned too far over..." I gave him a smile. "I was going to take you up in it today, actually."

"The helicopter?" he asked. "You have one here?"

"Yep, lots of stations have 'em for mustering out here. Mine's just a secondhand one, but it goes real good."

Travis looked a little surprised. "You want to take me up in it?"

"Yep. It's good for you to see the land from above, landmarks, that kind of thing. It's hard to gauge distances from the ground, but when we're mustering next week, it'll give you a better understanding of where you are and where we need to go."

"Okay. Cool."

After all necessary checks on the helicopter, Travis was

excited as we climbed into the small chopper. "It's a Robinson R22," I told him. "Thought you might recognise them actually. They're American made."

He put on a headset. "Some of the big ranches have these, but not where I'm from."

"Been in one before?" I asked. He shook his head, and I grinned at him. "Don't worry, we're not mustering today so no fancy moves or death-defying stops, rolls or turns."

His eyes shot to mine and I laughed. "I said we *won't* be doing that," I said, putting on my headset. "Can you hear me?" I asked, looking at him.

His voice sounded in my headset. "Depends. Are you gonna kill me in this?"

I laughed again. "I'll take it easy on ya." He looked at me disbelievingly. "I won't do anything!" I said again. It probably didn't help that I laughed yet again. "I don't wanna clean vomit off the dash."

With a wave to George, I took the chopper up; Travis's smile got wider the higher I went. Normally when mustering we'd stick close to the ground—the skips would be just a metre or so off the tops of the trees and saltbush—but not today. I took us up about ten metres and headed north.

I loved flying. Yes, it was a faster mustering method that saved me hundreds of man-hours, but it was where I could really see the station for what it was: vast, very red, mostly arid, peppered with patches of gum trees and saltbush, rocky outcrops and ridges; it was beautiful.

"Wow," Travis said. I don't know if he meant to say it out loud, but I heard him through my headset.

"I know," I agreed. "Isn't she beautiful?"

"It really is," he said, looking at me. His smile was huge, as were his eyes.

"Beautiful, and equally brutal," I said. "This land has left more men broken than bull-riding ever could."

He looked at me and smiled, and it was like he wanted to say something, but didn't. Instead, he looked out his side window. "Yeah, I'd imagine so," he mumbled.

We rode in silence for a while, the vast spans of red dirt passing underneath the glass floor of the chopper. I wondered what he was going to say, but had chosen not to. I wondered why he didn't say it. I almost asked him, but figured it was best to keep conversation along the lines of why we were up here.

"Over this ridge up here," I said, pointing up ahead of us, "we'll see the start of the herd. There's a bit of gorge that runs through here. It's actually Arthur River. Only runs when it rains. The cattle'll migrate toward it from farther north when it gets too dry up there. Last month we closed the top paddocks to bring 'em down. Makes it easier for us, so we don't have to bring 'em in from the tops. We'll still have to do a run for any stragglers, but by the end of the dry season they'll come down for water."

"And it's the end of the dry season now?"

"Yeah, comin' into what the locals call the build-up," I said. "When it gets humid as hell before the rains break."

"And that's why it's so hot?"

I laughed. "This isn't hot. It's only mid-thirties. But it's gonna get hot these next few weeks." Then I said, "Hey, I thought our temperatures were pretty similar."

"They are, though it gets hotter here. I looked up what I could expect before I got here." Then he added, "Not like that poor English guy ya'll talked about last night."

I snorted. "Yeah, apparently it wasn't pretty."

"You weren't here then?" he asked. I think he was trying to act casual.

I almost didn't answer him; after all, I was used to being private and I barely knew this man. But in the end, I said, "I was in Sydney." I wasn't going to elaborate on that, but thought I'd already said that much, I figured why bloody not. "I was at uni. It was a bachelor of agricultural science at the University of Sydney." To my right, I spotted one of the water troughs and hooked the chopper around so we could land. I figured it would be a good distraction and seeing how he handled himself around cattle seemed like a good idea.

I landed the chopper a safe distance from the small corrugated iron shed that housed the bore that fed the water trough, and we walked toward it. I explained the gravity-fed bore and as we walked between cattle, he never hesitated. He was completely comfortable and he knew what he was doing. I was relieved, and surprised.

And happy.

I don't know why it made me happy. I guess I didn't want to see him fail out here, especially in front of the other guys, and seeing he could handle his own made me smile.

We checked the bore, and when we climbed back into the chopper, I said, "There's another one I want to check."

He slipped off the hat I'd given him and put the headset on again. When we were up in the air again, he looked around. "How far does your property go?"

"See the horizon?"

Travis looked out the windscreen of the helicopter. "Yeah."

"About three hundred kilometres past that."

Travis shook his head and let out a disbelieving laugh. "I knew it was big...but jeez. You know, 2.58 million acres looks big on paper and you *know* it's big, but to see it? It's huge!"

"We're not the biggest out here," I told him.

"Third biggest in the state," he said.

"Territory," I corrected him with a smile. "We're not a state."

"Sorry, Northern *Territory*," he amended. "Eighth biggest station in the country."

"You did your research."

"I did a bit before coming out here, yeah. My momma needed to know where I was going," he said.

"Sutton Station is ten thousand, four hundred and sixty square kilometres. We have a stock rate of eight-to-ten."

His eyes widened. "That's twenty-five hundred head of cattle!"

"And we bring 'em in twice a year," I told him with a smile, impressed that he worked out the figures in his head so quickly. I'd have needed a calculator. Then something caught my eye. "Look down there," I said, pointing to my right. I leaned the controls to follow my line of sight and so Travis could get a better look at the mob of kangaroos in full flight over the red dirt.

He leaned forward a bit, and when he looked back at me, his grin was almost from ear to ear. "Holy shit, they're fast," he said. "That's awesome!"

"I should tell the boys. But we're a bit far out," I said. Travis looked at me, waiting for me to explain. "They shoot them."

"You shoot kangaroos?"

"Yep. Bloody pests," I said. He looked kind of stunned. "What? Don't they tell you that in the tourism brochures?"

He shook his head. "Ah, no."

"We'll use the meat for dog food. Sometimes the boys'll eat it if they're out droving for a time, but it's gotta be cooked right or you'd be better off eatin' an old boot."

"Hmm," he said, and his lips formed a flat, watery line. "I think I'll stick to beef and lamb, thanks."

I laughed. "After a few days drovin' you'll be so tired and hungry you won't care about what you're eatin'."

"I'll have to take your word on that," he said.

"You'll find out next week. We'll be out here on horseback," I said as I put the chopper down near the next bore. "Hope you're good for a week in the saddle."

He smiled and nodded as he got out of the helicopter. "I'm sure I am."

As we walked up to the tin shed that housed the pump to the bore, I stopped him. "Grab a shovel."

"What for?" he asked. "What the hell are we digging out here?"

"The shovel's not for digging. It's a snake repellent."

Travis's expression was a mix of *oh shit* and *what the fuck*. "Repellent?"

"Yep. If you see one, cut its head off."

He paled a little. "You know, I read up on all the deadly animals you got out here. Brown snakes, taipans, tiger snakes, not to mention the spiders." He swallowed hard. "I'm guessing you don't have antivenin handy and we're—" He looked at his watch. "—ooooh, a mere three hours and hello-complete-respiratory-failure from the hospital..."

I smiled at him and held out the shovel. "So when you hit one, don't miss." I chuckled. "Anyway, it's more of a blood coagulation issue before the respiratory problem."

He snatched the shovel. "You're not funny, asshole."

Well, the fact that the venom makes your blood turn to soup wasn't funny, but the look on his face was funny as hell. I even ignored the name calling. "Come on," I told him. "I'll go first."

We checked the bore, which was thankfully snake-free,

and then he checked out one or two of the Brahman that were standing close by the water trough. After that we headed back to the homestead. I pointed out landmarks we'd see along the way when droving and told him likely camping stops, depending on how the herd were travelling.

The plan would be I'd take the helicopter, and Bacon, Fish, Ernie, Trudy and Billy would head out north on Monday morning on horseback and motorbikes. George would take the Land Rover out Tuesday and again on Wednesday with fresh supplies, then I'd go back with George on Wednesday afternoon to fly the helicopter up as far north as needed to bring down the last of the cattle to meet up with the rest of the herd.

The crew on horseback and bike would start to bring them down, I'd come back with fresh supplies and resume on horseback until we were back at the holding yards.

Then I'd take the helicopter back out for one last round up, with a few guys on horseback and dirt bike to bring in any cattle that went astray.

Overall from start to finish, it'd take a week.

"You'll be with the droving team," I told him. "Heading out with us first thing Monday after next."

Travis grinned. "Cool!"

"We'll need to see how you go on horseback or bike first," I said. "It's nothing personal. I just need to see how you handle both, 'cause when you're out there in the middle of nowhere, there's not much room for error."

"It's fine," he said with a smug smile. "I understand that. And anyway, I can handle both okay."

We landed back at the station, and after we unloaded the few emergency supplies we took with us and completed the safety checks and flight log, I suggested Travis take one of the dirtbikes for a spin.

He wheeled the bike out to where me and George were waiting and swung his leg over the bike. My mind fell to the gutter with how his jeans hugged his ass and thighs and the way he straddled the bike. I pretended to find a loose thread on my shirt interesting until he kick-started the bike, turned the wheel and sprayed red dust all over me and George.

George sputtered and brushed himself down. "What the hell was that for?" he coughed.

I spat the dust out of my mouth. "I may have questioned his ability to ride."

George snorted and clapped my shoulder. "Well, consider yourself answered."

"Hmm," I grumbled. "Smug fucking Yank."

CHAPTER THREE

SMUG FUCKING YANK. YEP. I SAID IT.

GEORGE BURST OUT LAUGHING. "Right, smug. Is that what they're calling it these days?" he said with a laugh. I eyed him questioningly, and he smiled. "That smug fucking Yank has held your attention all day."

I raised one eyebrow at him. "I showed him an aerial view of where he'll be droving next week."

"He's coming on the drovin' run?" George asked.

"Yep. I took him out to the second bore and he stuck his hands straight in and was liftin' pipes. Didn't think twice. He knew what he was doing. And with the Brahman, he just walked right up to 'em and knew where to touch 'em, where to stand. He's a farmer, George. I ain't got no problem with him coming."

George gave a hard nod. "I'll make plans. We'll need to prep another bike or horse, gear, food... I better let Ma know there'll be another mouth to feed."

"I'll let Ma know," I said. "I have some calls to make inside, but after lunch I'll leave Travis with you. He can get his own gear ready for Monday, just like everyone else."

"Fair enough."

We stood and watched as Travis rode slowly back to us. We could see his smile from where we were. "And get him to bring in the Bay gelding. We'll see if he's as smug on a horse as he is on a bike."

After lunch and some business phone calls later, I could hear George laughing outside. I followed the sound to the back door of the homestead, and obviously hearing the same laughter as I did, Ma came in and stood beside me.

Travis was saddling up the horse, but must have said something funny to George. They were both smiling. Travis obviously knew his way around a horse, he was buckling up the girth and lengthening stirrups while he was talking to and looking at George.

"He's a nice boy," Ma said. "Cute too, don't ya think?"

"Ma, please," I cautioned. "We've been through this."

"Don't write him off yet," she said. "Do you know which team he bats for?"

"Ma," I hissed. "It's not like that. It's professional."

"And talking on the front porch all night," she said casually. "Was that you just being *professional*?"

I sighed.

"That's what I thought," she said.

I amended my earlier comment. "Ma, it *can't* be like that."

"Why not?"

"He's a guest here. I'm responsible for him. You know there are rules about business and pleasure."

"Maybe it's your responsibility to provide both..."

I pushed out through the screen door before she even finished *that* sentence, and bounded down toward the holding yard where George stood watching Travis.

Jesus. He'd only been here a day.

I mean, it hadn't been *that* long since I'd been with

someone... I tried to remember the last time I'd had sex... okay, so going on a year and a half was probably too long.

Fucking hell.

I walked down to where George stood, kinda pissed at myself. I leaned against the holding yard railing and put one booted foot on the bottom rail.

"You okay?" George asked quietly.

He could always read me. "Yeah." I looked over at him and gave him a smile and a pat on the shoulder. "I'm good." But then Travis, who'd been standing, talking quietly to the horse, gripped the horn of the saddle, put his left foot in the stirrup and hoisted himself up into the seat.

The horse turned in a circle and Travis's arms flexed, the muscles in his forearms bulging as he kept the reins tight. His jeans hugged his thighs and ass as he lifted his hips in the saddle.

I bit back a groan and put my head down, resting my forehead on the railing.

"You got him," George called out to him, meaning he had full control of the horse.

Travis laughed, making me look up at him. He was grinning as he walked the gelding around the yard. If there were any horses that might have given him grief it was this gelding, yet he had the horse under full command.

George opened the gate and Travis led the gelding out, starting out in an easy trot as he headed down the driveway. He had a fluid motion, rising in the saddle, using his legs— almost standing in the stirrups—leaning over the neck of the animal, as he urged the horse to break into a gallop.

"Don't think you need to worry if the boy can ride," George said, laughing beside me. "Smug Yank, huh?"

I smiled and let out a heavy sigh. "Tell him not to bother getting off. I'll go saddle up. He'll have the gelding all riled up, riding him like that. We may as well head out on horseback."

George gave a nod, but it looked like he was trying not to smile. I considered telling him to mind his own, but turned and walked away instead.

I grabbed my saddle from the shed, walked over to the housing paddock and slung the saddle over the fence. I stuck two fingers in my mouth and gave a loud whistle before walking back into the shed.

I heard Travis ride back in, and George telling him to stay on the horse.

"Told ya'll I could ride," Travis said, his accent thick. Then after a second, he said, "What did Charlie whistle for?"

"Callin' his horse," George replied.

"Callin' his what?" Travis asked.

I smiled to myself as I grabbed the bridle and headed back out toward my saddle, and sure enough, just like always, Shelby came galloping in. She was a buckskin, kind of small for a stockhorse, but the best I'd ever seen. She lifted her head and snorted a few times, stomping the ground with her front leg.

I climbed through the fence and ran my hand along her neck and down her shoulder. I let her smell me and nudge me, like she always did. "Hey, girl," I said softly. "Been a few days, huh?"

She nudged me again with her forehead, so I rubbed her ears and let her rest her head on my shoulder. Ignoring the eyes I could feel on me, I slipped on the bridle, then threw over the rug and saddle. I quickly strapped it up, put my left foot in the stirrup and threw my right leg over, and settled into the saddle. When I pulled the reins, we turned to find Travis and George watching me. Travis was keeping the unsettled gelding in line, pulling on the reins, but he never took his eyes off me.

George was grinning from ear to ear. He shook his head, so I threw him the water canister, which he caught easily. He filled it with water from the tap at the trough and tossed it back to me, then opened the gate for Travis.

George, the man who'd been like a father to me, looked up at me, not even trying to hide his smile. "Don't be too late now."

Before I could chip him, Travis rode the gelding in and Shelby threw her head back, making me pull hard and turn her around. When I looked back at George, the gate was shut and he was walking away.

"She alright?" Travis asked, nodding toward Shelby.

"She's fine," I told him. I gave her a nudge with my toes. "Yah," I called, and Shelby took flight.

I looked back to find Travis not too far behind me. Yeah, he could ride well, but I was better. Especially with Shelby. She was a beautiful mare, smart as hell. I loved being out here with her. I trusted her judgment and there weren't too many people or animals on the planet that I could say that about.

I rode her flat out for a few hundred metres and slowly started to pull her up, letting her run herself out. Travis was alongside me in no time and we slowed to a walk.

He was still grinning, but he settled into the saddle. "It's really beautiful here," he said. "I was expecting it to be a lot like the deserts of Utah or Arizona, but it's really not. It looks more..." He trailed off, like he couldn't find the right word.

"Australian?" I finished for him.

He laughed. "Exactly. But it sure is pretty."

I snorted at him. "You wanna be careful or this red dirt

will get into your blood." Then I pointed over toward the western fence line. "We'll follow that," I told him. We led the horses over to the trees near the far western fence and followed the line for a while. I explained how this would be one of the holding yards when the cattle came down. We dismounted in the shade of some trees and Travis threw the loose reins over the fence. I let Shelby's reins hang loose.

"Not much shade out here," Travis noted.

I laughed. "Not much grows tall enough to produce it."

He crouched down and scooped up a handful of the dirt at his feet. "It's the reddest soil I've seen."

"It's like sand," I told him. "Poor filtration, no nutrition."

"Some of the toughest farming conditions on the planet," he said, looking up at me.

I ran my hand down Shelby's neck. "Does that make me crazy?"

Travis laughed and stood up, letting the red sand fall through his fingers. "It's incredible."

I looked at him now like he was crazy.

"It is!" he cried. "Absolutely incredible," he said again, quieter this time, almost in wonder. He went on to talk about the soil types and geological bases of his parents' farm back in Texas. I'd forgotten that he was a student, or rather, had *been* a student. He'd technically finished studying—but still, I was reminded by the way he described the alkaline clays and sandy loams of his hometown that not only was he here to learn, but he also loved what he did.

And the way he used his hands when he spoke animatedly was really distracting. His big hands, thick fingers and callused palms... I kept thinking about what they'd feel like on my skin...

Needing a distraction, I turned to Shelby, suddenly rather interested in her mane. I hadn't noticed that Travis had stopped talking until he was standing right beside me. "She's a special horse," he stated. It wasn't a question.

I cleared my throat. "She is." He waited for me to keep talking, so I did. "I got her when she was just a foal, jeez, it'd be eight years ago. When I was sixteen and seventeen, we were inseparable. She was my best friend. Then I left her for three years and when I came back from Sydney, she came over to me and nudged me right into the fence. I think she was pissed that I left her," I said with a laugh. "But she forgave me."

Like she knew I was talking about her, she nudged me, softly this time.

Travis chuckled beside me. "I think she likes you."

I looked at him and grinned. "She's saved my hide a few times. Whether it was shying away from snakes or after I'd have a fight with my dad, I'd go sit up at one of my hideouts and she'd nudge me until I took her home."

Travis smiled warmly, as though it sounded familiar. "I thought whistling for horses only happened in the movies."

I laughed loudly. "Paddocks are pretty big out here." Then I asked him, "Got a horse back home?"

"Nah, not really. I mean, we have two horses, but they're my sisters'. I grew up with one, that's where I learned to ride, but it's been a few years. It felt real good to be on this fella," he said, rubbing the forehead of the bay gelding. "What's his name?"

"Never gave him one," I admitted. "We have a few horses 'round here. He was a bit of a problem one and weren't sure if he was going on one of the trucks at the end of the muster."

"You put me on a *problem horse?*"

I laughed at his expression. "Had to see if you could ride."

"Gee, thanks," he said. He rolled his eyes, but smirked.

"You handled him well."

Travis gave the gelding a pat down the neck. "He's not getting on that truck the week after next."

I looked at him surprised. "No?"

He shook his head. "Nah. Not while I'm here, anyway."

I scoffed at his arrogance, but he stared at me. His blue eyes were smiling, challenging.

"And I get to name him," he added. Then he frowned, obviously trying to think of a name. "Umm... I can't think of anything significant."

"What about Her Majesty's Service?" I asked, biting back a smile.

"Huh?"

"You know, the British armed forces," I explained. "Always carrying the Americans."

His mouth literally fell open and I burst out laughing, startling the gelding. When I finally stopped laughing, Travis was still staring at me. Well, it was more glaring at me.

I laughed some more. "Do you get it? The horse carries you, and you're American."

"I get it," he said. "Just not funny."

"It really was. What about James Bond? Or Mi6."

Now he rolled his eyes. "How about I call him Texas. Just to peeve you off."

I laughed again and clapped him on the shoulder. "That's perfect! Texas is perfect for this horse. He thinks he's the biggest too."

Travis sighed. "Is it National Pick on the American Day today? 'Cause that weren't in no travel brochure either."

I snorted out a laugh. "I'm just kidding," I said, clapping

him on the arm this time. "I don't mean nothing by it. It's just what we do. We take the piss."

"Take the piss?"

"Yeah, make fun of. It wasn't real nice, sorry." I kind of felt bad, but it also felt real damn good to laugh. I slipped my foot into the stirrup and climbed back onto Shelby. "We'll just check the bore farther down this fence line. We'll need these troughs working well next week."

I pulled the reins, turning Shelby out of the shade and down along the fence line. I don't know why making conversation was so fucking hard or why I struggled so damn pathetically. Now Travis thought I was a jerk, and I was supposed to be his boss. I was supposed to be someone he could depend upon, not someone who took the piss.

It really was safer for me to just talk work or not talk at all.

Travis was soon beside me again on the newly named Texas. "We'll draft the mob into these two paddocks, then section them off again," I said, getting back to much safer topics. "Bulls into one pen and steers into another pen, females and wieners into the other. We'll see which of each we'll keep, which we'll sell."

"You didn't offend me, you know."

I glanced at him. He was smiling that smug half smirk. I cleared my throat and said, "I, uh, I still shouldn't have said that. And I apologise."

"You wanna know what else we have in Texas?" he asked, ignoring my apology. "We have a sense of humour. I mean, they did a pretty thorough strip search at customs, but I'm pretty sure I smuggled mine in."

I smiled at that. "Was it bad? Customs, I mean."

"Oh, terrible. Questioned for hours, strip searched, cavity searched."

My eyes near popped out of my head. "Really?"

"No," he answered flatly, but then he laughed.

I chuckled and shook my head. "Jeez, I thought you were being serious."

He grinned and gave a nod toward a water trough we were getting close to. "What number bore is this?" he asked. "What's your water table like?"

And just like that, we talked about underground water supplies, both here and where he was from, which led to talk about sustainability and desert living, cultivating every drop of water and irrigation and water harvesting.

He'd laughed when I said the only irrigation we do out here was once a year, and that we called it the wet season. We spent the entire afternoon walking the fence line, talking and laughing. He told me about his family—he had a brother and two sisters, both parents, who were still married. They did all right on the farm, he said, and he was the second youngest, which was fine with him. It meant all the responsibilities and expectations were on older brother and sister. "They can do the career, marriage, kids thing and I can do whatever I want."

"Like spend four weeks in the Outback of Australia?"

"Exactly," he said with a grin. Then he asked, "What about your family?"

I held in a sigh and kept the smile on my face. "Only child," I said. "I grew up out here." I looked around at the familiar, ever-changing scenery and where the sun was in the sky. I looked at my watch. "Shit. We'll be late for dinner. Come on," I said, quickly jumping back on Shelby. "Ma's number one rule is don't be late."

Travis was quick to get on Texas, and he mumbled my earlier words. "Be on time, be clean, be grateful."

Smiling, I gave Shelby a nudge with my toes, telling her

to head for home, and she took off. Travis wasn't far behind, laughing as he rode. By the time we got back to the homestead, we were both sweating, as were the horses. I jumped off Shelby and quickly undid the girth, pulling the saddle off her and throwing it onto the fence railing. Travis did the same, and we led both horses over to the shade of the shed. I grabbed the hose and wet the horses down and Travis grabbed both saddles and brought them into the shed. "You should go in and get cleaned up for dinner. Ma won't mind too much if it's me that's late."

Travis gave me a smile before he took off to the house. I couldn't help but laugh as he hopped on one foot on the veranda, tryin' to take his boots off, then disappeared inside.

I don't know why he disarmed me so much. He was probably straight for all I knew, and as I knew from past experience, that fantasy never ended well.

I gave the horses a good hosing, washing the dirt and sweat off them. I left them tied to the fence in the shade and went inside.

I hung my hat on the second hook and saw the hat I'd given to Travis sitting on the hallstand. I ducked in through the door off the hall that led past my bedroom and went straight to the bathroom. Travis wasn't there, but I could tell he'd been there. There was water over the basin with traces of red dirt swirled to the drain.

It made me smile.

I scrubbed up as quick as I could and went back down the hall toward the dining room, but when I got to the door, I could hear them talking.

"You actually heard him laugh?" someone asked. It sounded like Ernie.

Then an American accent. "Laugh? He almost busted something he laughed so hard."

"Did you fall off your horse?" Trudy asked. "'Cause he finds that funny."

I almost didn't want to go in. I hesitated in the hall just as Ma came out with the bread rolls. "Ooooh, just in time," she said, pretending to scowl at me. "Quick, in ya go."

I walked in and silence fell over the table. It was just as well Ma followed me in. She put the bread on the table and then everyone was eating, so there was no conversation anyway. I could feel Travis's eyes on me, but I didn't look at him.

All through dinner, his gaze burned into me. I could almost feel the questions.

Why haven't you ever laughed with them?
The way you did with me today?
Why don't you show them?
Why do you act different around me?

"Isn't that right, Charlie?" Bacon asked.

"Huh?" I said. I put my fork down on my empty plate, looking at him. "Sorry, I didn't hear what you said."

"This weekend, in the Alice," he repeated. He was grinning. "Young Travis here was sayin' he didn't think he should go. We was just telling him he should; we'll show him how us Territorians do it."

Was it a good idea? Did I want him to go out drinking with these guys for a weekend? Maybe hearing stories of his women conquests might get rid of these ludicrous ideas I had in my head about him.

I finally looked at Travis. "You should go."

CHAPTER FOUR

PLAN A. AND POSSIBLY PLAN B. THERE
COULD BE A C, DEPENDING ON HOW
EPICALLY I FAIL AT PLANS A AND B.

I WAS UP and out of the house before dawn, putting in an hour's work before breakfast. I told George that Travis was with Trudy, Mick and Billy for the day. Thankfully George's only response was a hard nod and not the implied innuendos he was full of the day before.

Fish and Bacon were servicing the dirt bikes, and I kept myself busy under the Land Rover all day.

I avoided Travis as much as I could without being rude. I was just being professional. The questions I asked myself last night at dinner, and the subsequent answers, were true. I shouldn't treat him any differently.

So last night after dinner, I brushed down the two horses and turned them out, then spent an hour or two in my office with the door shut.

Even at breakfast and lunch, I kept eye contact to a minimum, but smiled so he wouldn't think he'd done anything wrong.

Dinner was full of talk about the team's weekend off, and what they'd do when they got into Alice Springs. I just smiled along with them all, ignoring the quick glances from Travis and the long, drilling looks from George.

The next morning, as much as I'd tried to distract myself from the blue-eyed American, as I rounded the hall on my way to the bathroom, I ran right into him.

Literally.

"Sorry," I started.

He had his towel in his hand, his short brown hair still damp; he smelled all shower-clean and of toothpaste-mint. "Oh, hey," he said, startled. Then he said, "Um, look, if I did something..."

"What?"

He swallowed hard. "It's just you've hardly spoken a word to me since the other day. If I crossed a line, I just wanted to say I was sorry—"

"You haven't done anything wrong," I cut him off.

He stared at me for a long moment, and I had to look away. "Alright then," he said quietly. "Look, if you don't want me to go away with the others this weekend—"

"You should," I answered quickly. "Go into town. Have some fun."

"Charlie?" Ma called from around the hall. "You alive in there?" I took a reflexive step back, away from Travis, toward the bathroom. "Oh, there you are. Always a worry when you're not under my feet sniffin' for breakfast."

"Just cleanin' up, Ma," I said, stepping into the bathroom and closing the door behind me.

"Right, then," I heard her say. "Travis, you can set the table for me."

"Yes, ma'am" was his reply, and I heard Ma laugh all the way back to her kitchen.

I stood at the basin and splashed cold water on my face. I needed to get my shit together. Seriously. He'd been here all of four days, and he was all I could think about. His eyes, his accent, the way he laughed, the line of his neck. Jesus, he was the reason I barely slept the last two nights. It was getting ridiculous.

I scrubbed my hands with soap and told the man in the mirror the same words his father had said.

"No fucking fairy will run this station. It takes a man's man to survive out here."

I'd said the words out loud before I could stop them.

Those fucking words.

I don't know how, but I'd almost convinced myself I wasn't the disappointment my father thought I was. After these last two years back on the farm with no prospective guys in a few hundred kilometre radius, I was almost convinced I wasn't gay or straight or anything. I'd resigned to living a life of solitude, like my father, in the middle of the Outback.

I splashed more water over my face, avoiding making eye contact with myself in the mirror again. I wiped my face on the towel, and with a reinforced determination, I went out to the dining room.

I took my seat just as Ma was finishing up serving, with George on one side and Travis on the other. Everyone was excited today; they were heading off in a few hours for their weekend of god-knows-what. I kept my head down, smiling as they talked, and avoided looking at Travis directly.

I only had to get through breakfast, then he'd be gone for the weekend and I'd be fine. But just before we were all done, Ma stood in the doorway. "Charlie, a word in the kitchen?"

I suppressed a sigh, and George chuckled beside me. "Boy, what have you done?"

Without a word, I pushed my chair back and stood up, then walked out of the dining room and into the kitchen.

Ma was at the sink, but she turned around to face me. Her eyes were soft and kind of sad. "Charlie, are you okay?"

"I'm fine, why?"

"When I walked into the hall," she said. "I hope I didn't interrupt anything."

"Ma," I said with a sigh. "It's not like that."

"The look on your face," she said quietly. "You looked like a scared rabbit, tis all."

"Gee, thanks," I mumbled.

"You ain't got nothing to be scared of, 'kay, hun?"

"Ma," I said, changing the subject completely, needing this conversation to be over. "When was the last time George took you out for dinner?"

She was confused for a second, and I could tell the moment she knew our discussion about me was over. "What? You mean pay for someone else to cook? Joseph Brown has never."

I smiled at her. "Then you know what? You both should go into Alice with the rest of them. Two nights in a motel, and I'll tell George you get to pick the restaurants, and I'll pay for it."

She smiled, but then she softened. "You don't need to send us away. You just need to ask for some alone time."

"I'm asking for some alone time," I admitted. "But I want you and George to enjoy some time away too, okay? You deserve it. You've done more for me than anyone else ever has."

"Oh." Her eyes glistened. "Sweet boy," she said, pulling me in for a hug. Then she stepped back with wide eyes. "You're not getting rid of us, are you?"

I snorted. "I can't run this place without you. Without either of you. You need to be back on Sunday, okay?"

Ma smiled at me in that motherly way she does. "What will you do?"

"The usual."

"I meant about our guest."

"Nothing," I answered. "I don't know what you mean."

She sighed. "Are you just going to ignore him until he leaves?"

"That's plan A, yes," I admitted and then thankfully was saved by George appearing in the doorway. "George! Just the man I wanted to see. I'm giving you and Ma the weekend off. I'll book you into some fancy motel, and you can take your girl out for dinner. Let someone else cook for her for a change."

George blinked. Then he blinked again. "Uh..."

"It's settled," I told them. "I'll find you a nice place to stay and pay for it over the phone. You just need to go get packed."

George looked at Ma, then back to me. "Did I miss something?"

"Nothing you need to worry yourself about," Ma told him. "Just finish up your chores already." She started to lecture him about what to pack, what not to pack, then to just forget packing altogether; it'd be better left to her. That was my cue. I clapped him on the shoulder as I walked out, and I could feel his eyes burning holes into the back of my head until I walked outside.

I spent the rest of the morning, until they all left, implementing plan A.

THE HOUSE WAS QUIET. It hadn't been this quiet since I arrived back here for my father's funeral. There really hadn't been a time since then that there hadn't been someone else here, usually Ma or George, or any of my workers. Sure, I had enough time by myself when I was out checking fences or bores and most nights when Ma and George had gone to bed. But this was two whole days with the nearest human being was a few hundred kilometres away.

God, I needed this.

I hadn't realised just how much I needed some alone time until I said it out loud to Ma. I'd booked and paid for two nights in a hotel for them and told them to charge any restaurant bills back to the room and the hotel would take it off my credit card.

I'd said goodbye to them all as they were leaving, still not managing to make eye contact with Travis. I'd set about doing my afternoon work, fed the animals and tidied up the shed and finally came inside when my stomach told me it was dinner time.

I opened the fridge door to find containers of food premade by Ma. I smiled despite the insult that she thought I was too useless to cook for myself. I took one marked 'dinner' out of the fridge and threw it in the microwave. I went and got cleaned up, but when the microwave beeped, instead of taking dinner to the table, I sat on the lounge, in front of the TV and put my feet up on the coffee table.

Television out here wasn't great; when I was a kid, it was so bad I would hardly ever watch it. But now with the introduction of satellite TV and the internet, I could pretty much watch what I wanted.

I scanned through the movie channels, hoping for some foreign gay film, but settled on a rerun of Die Hard. After

John McLean had yippee-ki-yay'd every mother fucker, I grabbed my laptop out of my office, turned the lights off and went to my room.

I could have done this at my office desk or even on the sofa, but jerking off to gay porn where Ma did the daily crossword kind of weirded me out.

I needed to get Travis out of my head. I had two days to get rid of any silly ideas, foolish notions or fantasies out of my system, and what better way to do that than to watch men fuck.

Men that didn't have short brown hair, cool blue eyes and American accents.

I stripped off my clothes, grabbed some hand lotion and tissues, and, leaning up against my headboard with my laptop on my thighs, started trolling the usual sites.

I was already hard, so I put my laptop beside me and pressed play. It didn't matter which video I watched at this point. I just needed to watch something. I quickly applied some lotion to my hand and gripped myself, watching the men on screen kiss at first, their ripped bodies, naked and beautiful. Unable to wait, I skipped the lovey-dovey shit and prepping scenes and went straight for the fucking. All I needed to see was the cock slipping into an ass, balls tight, and the moaning. Fuck, I needed to hear the moaning.

The bottom threw his head back and groaned as he took an entire cock into his ass, and that was all it took.

My cock surged in my hand, my hips flexed one last time and I came. Hot strips of cum poured onto my stomach, down my hand, and my head spun as my orgasm rocked through me.

By the time I could focus on the laptop screen, the two guys were covered in cum and kissing. I wiped myself clean with some tissues and still needing more, I clicked on the next video.

I watched from the beginning this time while languidly stroking my cock back to life. It didn't take long. I watched the men on screen, kissing, naked, missionary. I missed that intimacy. Someone to hold me, touch me, kiss me.

My strokes became harder, twisting my hand over the head of my cock while imagining it was me being kissed like that. That it was my cock buried in that ass while he kissed me like that, moaned for me like that.

That it was Travis who begged me like that.

My eyes shot open and my hand stopped. My cock was aching and throbbing in protest.

With my other hand, I clicked off that video and onto a new one. I didn't even wait for it to start; I just clicked two-thirds into the clip. I didn't want to watch them kiss and touch, I just needed to watch them fuck.

The video started at a scene with one guy on his hands and knees and three guys behind him. They took turns fucking him, each sliding their dicks in, pumping a few times and then letting the other guys do the same.

It was pig-dirty, there was no emotion to it, it was just pure animal-need fucking. And it was hot.

After a few rounds, the next guy kept thrusting, fucking until he came all over the guy's ass.

My orgasm rolled through my belly, building.

The next guy moved in, sliding in easily. I stroked harder, imagining it was me. The man on screen fucked the ass in front of him, until he pulled out at the last minute, spraying cum over the bottom's hole.

My cock swelled and my balls tightened. The building pleasure coiled tight in every cell of my body.

Then on screen the next guy took his turn. His big, fat

cock pushed in deep, making both men moan loudly. The sound sent warm shivers over my skin. He gripped the hips in front of him, driving in every inch over and over. The camera cut to a view from underneath, so all I could see was balls flush against ass, and the moaning got louder and the fucking got harder. Only this guy didn't pull out, he thrust in one last time, his balls drew up and he came deep in the guy's ass.

My orgasm ripped from my toes, sending flashes of white hot pleasure through my entire body as my cock spilled hot bursts of cum over my stomach.

It took a little while for the room to stop spinning, but I closed my laptop, rolled off my bed and cleaned myself up in the shower.

I climbed back into bed, sleepy and sated. I refused to think about the last video I watched, how it was nothing but dirty porn.

Most of all, I refused to think about Travis.

But I woke up before the sun with dreams of a soft American accent whispering in my ear still swirling through my brain.

I squeezed my dick to stop the ache, but it made it worse.

I closed my eyes and had visions of his blue eyes fluttering closed and his head falling back as I pressed my lips to his neck. Then he pulled my face to his and kissed me, and I came again and again, my back arching off the bed as I fucked my fist.

Completely spent and boneless, I lay in bed trying to catch my breath.

Okay, this infatuation, this stupid fantasy, was officially getting ridiculous.

I jumped out of bed, cleaned myself up, pulled on some

shorts, stripped the sheets and stomped through the too-quiet house toward the laundry. I needed to be busy, I told myself. So I had a quick breakfast and kept myself busy. All damn day.

I stayed in and around the homestead. Not that I was short of transport. I mean, everyone had piled into the only two four-wheel drives to go to Alice Springs, but I still had five dirt bikes and a half a dozen horses I could ride. Hell, I even had the helicopter.

But being out here all by myself with the nearest help hours away, I didn't risk it. I'd never been this isolated. If a bike broke down or if I fell off a horse – not that I had since I was a kid – it could be a death sentence.

The temperature was over forty degrees Celsius and the humidity before the wet season was always hellish. If I got left a few hours from the homestead with no water and no one to come get me, it could kill me.

Rule number one of the Outback: Don't be an idiot.

I had plenty to do anyway. I checked and rechecked all food lists, fuel and water supplies and medical kits for the first of the droving runs come Monday. I finished some laundry – I always did my own. Ma did everything else, but never anyone else's washing. Not that it bothered me, I mean, I was a grown man, I could do my own. I swept and mopped the floors, fed the animals, did a few hours in the office and not once did I think about *him*.

Not until I got into bed anyway.

I'd eaten dinner in front the TV again, watched some lameass robot movie and turned it off before it even finished, and went to bed. I didn't need porn tonight. I recalled one of my many drunken college nights, dancing with strangers and having sex with them in bathroom stalls, backrooms, hotel rooms, dorm rooms.

I could remember the feeling of having the warm body of some guy underneath me as I sunk my cock into his ass. Those memories, a blur of strobing lights and alcohol, were all I had to fuel a life of solitude. I had them all stored in my mind and ready to recall when needed.

Only tonight, the memory wasn't of some random faceless stranger underneath me. As I jerked off—again—short brown hair and blue eyes appeared in my mind. His lips were parted in pleasure, his groans and whispers were laced with a Texan twang.

It wasn't some nameless man whose hands touched my face, bringing me in for a kiss. It was Travis.

And when I imagined my tongue in his mouth, the hand around my cock pumped harder, and reaching farther my other hand cupped my balls and one finger teased my hole before pressing inside.

"Fuck!" I cried as I came. My heart was hammering in my chest, my bones were spongy and my blood warmed through.

Sleepily, I cleaned myself up, throwing the tissues on the floor to deal with in the morning. I rolled over and pulled a pillow under my arm and for the briefest of moments, I wondered what it would be like to curl up and fall asleep with Travis in my arms.

My fantasies had officially left *this-is-getting-ridiculous* and had landed right in the middle of Crazytown.

***

I WOKE up the next morning feeling very removed.

If I dreamed of Travis I didn't remember. I rolled out of bed, then picked up the dried tissues off the floor and put them in the garbage, feeling more than a little pissed off with myself.

How I ever let it get to this was beyond me.

I needed to get my shit together. Everyone was due back this afternoon and I needed to have my fucking head screwed on straight.

Straight. Huh. How ironic.

If I wasn't so pissed off, that would be funny.

In no mood for breakfast, I did my early-morning chores. After the dogs and horses were fed, I headed back in for a shower.

And something got the better of me.

My father's fucking words.

I took my laptop with me and tried to watch some straight porn, like I'd tried a dozen times before, hoping it'd stir something in me – something to prove to the ghost of my father that I was someone he could be proud of.

Of course it didn't. I knew before I'd even started that it wouldn't. Sure, the guys in it were fit and hung, but the women were vocal, and even muted I still couldn't like it. I liked the grunts and groans of men in porn, and if watching porn was the extent of my sex life, I may as well as watch what I liked.

Which was men having sex with men.

As much as I wished it otherwise, I was gay. As much secondhand shame and disappointment I carried on behalf of my father, I couldn't change who I was.

I just chose to bury it.

I shut the laptop down, giving up on my plan A completely and even more pissed off with myself than before. Instead of opting for a shower, I pulled on my boots, grabbed my hat off the hook in the hall and a canister of water. The screen door slammed behind me, and walking over the fence, I whistled for Shelby.

CHAPTER FIVE

HE HAS A STAR TATTOO. OH, OF COURSE HE FUCKING DOES.

I RODE BACK into the yard and smiled when I saw the two Land Rovers parked out front. They were home. They were also early. I was hoping I'd be back before they got home. I rode Shelby to the water trough near the shed, and after jumping down, I unsaddled her and grabbed the hose.

She'd worked up a good sweat so I hosed her down, giving her a good rubdown for which she rewarded me with a nudge or two. I figured anyone inside the house would have seen or heard me, and I smiled at George when he walked out to see me.

"How was your weekend?" I asked him.

"Never mind me," he said. "Ma just about had a nervous breakdown when we got back and you weren't here."

"Ah, shit," I said. "I was hoping to be back before you."

"I told her if you weren't here by dinner we'd worry about panicking then," George said. "I figured I'd know where to find you anyway."

I smiled and nodded, silently admitting to where I'd been.

He raised one eyebrow. He knew I only went there to clear my head. "Everything okay?"

"Yeah," I answered, and then right on cue, the very reason for my bout of crazy walked out of the house and headed over. "Oh fuck." I didn't mean to say it out loud, even as a whisper. George's gaze shot to mine and he smiled.

"Well, you're alive," Travis said, walking over and petting Shelby's neck. He looked over my horse at me, all blue eyes and perfect smiles. "Ma had you snakebit and dying of thirst a hundred miles from home."

"Just went for a swim," I said as nonchalantly as I could. "Now I have to put Shelby in the holding yard."

Travis looked at me, then to the arid desert behind me. "A *swim*? Out there?"

I smiled. "Yeah, about thirty miles northeast."

His eyes popped wide. "Thirty miles? For a swim?"

"Spring-fed lagoon," I told him. "It's real pretty." Then I said, "How was your first weekend in the Alice with the crew?"

Travis groaned, and he looked at me most seriously. "They drink like fish. Actually, Fish, as in the man Fish, *is* a fish. He consumed more alcohol than oxygen. Which he's paying for now though, because he's as sick as a dog."

I chuckled. "You survived okay? Not hungover at all?"

"Actually, I feel terrible but don't tell any of them that. I'm trying to act all cool and shit, but really I feel like crap."

Despite my trying to not be affected by him, I burst out laughing, just as the screen door slammed and Ma came stomping over.

"Charles Sutton," she yelled, glaring at me as she walked. "You'll be the death of me."

Travis took a reflexive step back, I sighed and George

laughed as he took the reins from me, leading Shelby to the yard. I looked at Ma. "Oh, Ma," I said, using my you-could-never-hate-me tone. "I just went for a swim."

She put her hand on her hip. "You coulda left a note! I was worried about you being out there all by yourself."

I wrapped her up in a big bear hug and squeezed her 'til she squeaked. It was how I usually ended all our disagreements. I put her back down on the ground. "Ma, I've been out there a thousand times all by myself."

She just narrowed her eyes at me. "And what do you need to go all the way out there for to clear your head? The whole house was empty?"

I ignored that question—and the fact that Travis was still standing right beside me. "Now that you bring it up, how was *your* weekend away?" I asked, waggling my eyebrows at her. "George was a gentleman, I hope."

"Don't you answer that!" George called out from the holding yard.

"Gentleman?" Ma grinned, her eyes full of mischief. "That man's got the devil in him."

I snorted out a laugh, and even Travis chuckled at that. "How was the food?" I asked.

Ma tilted her head. "How did we go from talking about you to talkin' about me? I wasn't done yet!"

I gave her another hug. "I'm glad you had a great weekend, Ma."

She growled at me. "You get inside. The both of you. I have a list of things to do a mile long. Fancy sending me away the weekend before the season drove."

"We're organised," I told her.

"You might be, but I'm not," she said. "You can help me in the kitchen," she told me, then looked at Travis. "And you can do some laundry."

"Yes, ma'am," he said. I think she scared him.

"I'm a cook, not a slave," she added for good measure.

"Yes, ma'am."

"And quit callin' me ma'am. The name's Ma. Learn it. Use it."

Travis's wide eyes met mine, and I burst out laughing again. "Ma, leave him alone. You're scaring him."

"Bit of fear never hurt anyone," she said. Then she slid one arm around Travis and gave him a side-on hug. "Now, inside, both of you. I wasn't jokin' about doin' your own laundry."

NORMALLY A TIME OF RARE QUIET, dinner was loud. Even hungover, everyone was laughing and joking about their weekend away, telling stories of what they did and apparently what they didn't do.

"Not short on admirers this one," Bacon said, nodding to Travis. "Women lined up out the door almost." My stomach knotted; though I'd wanted him to go and have some fun, as it turns out, I didn't like hearing about it.

"Not quite," Travis said quietly, still cutting the meat on his plate, not looking up.

"Never took any of 'em up on their offer," Bacon went on.

"Not that we saw anyway," Fish added.

Travis shook his head. "Not my thing, really."

"Got a girl back home?" Fish asked. "Is that why?"

Travis swallowed hard and smiled. Then he shook his head. "Nah."

I was relieved. Fucking relieved. Can you believe that? God, I was pathetic.

"There was girls trippin' over 'emselves to talk to the *cute American*," Bacon said with a grin. "Weren't interested in us because of him."

"They weren't interested in you because you're a pig," Trudy said flatly.

"They don't call me Bacon for nothin'" he said, too thick to realise the insult.

The jokes and banter went around the table until there was no food left and Ma shooed us out. I helped Ma again in the kitchen She protested the entire time, but I told her shut up and deal with it.

She dropped the spatula into the sink with a loud clank and stared at me.

I just laughed. "The kitchen is neutral ground, remember?"

"Neutral ground is one thing, Charles Sutton," she said. "But tell me to shut up one more time and you'll be eating oatmeal three times a day."

"I hate oatmeal."

"Exactly."

"Point taken."

"Good, now get out of my kitchen."

"I thought you said you needed my help!"

"No, I really just wanted to get you and Travis inside together."

"Ma!"

"Oh what," she said, rolling her eyes. "They can't hear me. They're all outside. Where you should be. With him."

"Ma!"

"Out you go."

I sighed. "It's not like that."

"It could be," she said, putting her hands on my shoulders, turning me around and pushing me out of the kitchen. "Now what exactly have you got to lose?"

I snatched my hat off the hook and let the screen door slam behind me, hoping it would annoy Ma.

It could be.

What have I got to lose?

Ugh. That was the last thing I needed right now.

Billy saw me first. "Want me to go bring them horses in, boss?"

I nodded. "Yeah. Need a hand?"

Billy grinned at me, his smile huge and contagious despite my mood. He really didn't need anyone to help him; he and I both knew it. "If you want to, boss."

"I'll help him," Travis said. "I'm sure you're busy enough." He wasn't really asking for permission. He was already walking into the shed, to get a saddle, no doubt.

I liked that he was comfortable enough here to just jump right in. He fit in here. And I liked that more than I should.

I left them to it and did a few hours in the office instead. I'd lost track of time and the sound of laughter finally grabbed my attention. Not just anyone's laughter. A certain American's laughter.

I closed down my laptop and went to the front door. Travis, Billy and George were at the holding yard, and the three of them were laughing. I almost went out there, but instead stayed on the inside of the door, hidden. There was a lump of jealousy that he was laughing with them and not me, which was stupid. But there was also a heavy ache that felt a lot like loneliness.

"Sweetheart," Ma said softly, her hand on my shoulder. "What are you so afraid of?"

"I'm not afraid," I lied.

"Then what?"

"I don't even know if he's... if he's..." I couldn't even say it out loud.

"If he's gay?"

I hung my head. "Ma." I swallowed hard. "What if I say something... and what if he's not... interested."

She smiled sadly. "What if he is?"

I laughed at the absurdity of this whole fucking mess. I was in over my head, and he was oblivious. "It's stupid," I whispered.

"You need to ask him," Ma said. She patted my arm and left me looking out the door.

Only I didn't have to ask him at all.

Later that night when I was in bed, almost asleep, I heard the shower start. Soon after, when the water had shut off, I heard the bathroom door open so I got up to see if everything was okay and ran into Travis in the hall.

He was wearing nothing but a towel. I was wearing nothing but boxers.

I stood there like a rabbit in a spotlight, and a slow smile spread across his face. His gaze raked over my body, I swear I could feel it – like his eyes were warm hands skimming over my skin.

And there on his chest, right over his heart, was a single star. I knew what that symbol meant. "Is that a Texas star?" I asked, my voice cracking. I wanted him to say yes, hoped he'd say no.

He looked at me for a long moment, probably weighing up how to answer, what to give away, I realised. Then he shook his head slowly and bit his lip. "Not exactly."

"Good."

Good. I fucking said *good*.

"I um, I meant, *good*..." Because apparently saying once

wasn't bad enough, I fucking said it twice. And then because sheer mortification wasn't bad enough, I palmed my dick. I was getting hard. I did it without thinking, just needing some friction.

Travis's gaze followed my hand, and he smiled that smug goddamn smirk, then he looked back to the bathroom. "Did you need to use the bathroom?"

I shook my head. "No." So apparently I was also down to one-syllable words. I turned back to my door, wanting to shrink and die.

"Charlie," Travis said. I stopped and when I finally turned to face him, he was holding his clothes in front of his crotch. He looked right at me and took a deep breath like he was going to say something else. Instead he said, "Good night."

I nodded and quickly shut the door behind me, finally breathing. I stood leaning against the door, and I swear I heard him mutter, "Well, that answered that question."

Fuck.

CHAPTER SIX

I HARDLY SLEPT, tossing and turning all damn night, thinking of my encounter with Travis in the hall and how I'd face him in the morning.

Going back to my original plan A, which was to avoid him at all costs, I was up and out of the house early, getting most of my morning chores done before breakfast.

When Ma had hollered from the back door that if I didn't come in to eat right this instant, I could go ahead and starve, I seriously weighed up my options.

My stomach overruled my pride, and when I walked into the dining room, being the last one there, I took my seat and mumbled an apology for making them wait.

I didn't make eye contact with anyone, especially not the man sitting at my left. I could feel his gaze burning into me a few times from his seat barely a foot away, but I just kept my head down and ate my breakfast without a word. I know my mood usually put a damper on the rest of the table, so I grabbed a cup of tea on my way out and left them to it.

My silence, and the fact I'd been banging and clanging

around the shed an hour before the sun came up, was a pretty good warning to give me some space.

A fact someone forgot to tell Travis. Either that or he ignored it, because a little while later he followed me into the shed.

I was in the far corner, oiling saddles and bridles on the shelf along the back wall. He stood watching me for about a full minute while I pretended to ignore him. Eventually, it got the better of me. "Thought you were heading out with Billy today?"

"I am," he answered. "I have a suspicion that the boss is trying to get rid of me."

I stayed with my back to him and scrubbed the oiled cloth against the saddle harder. "Is that so?"

"Yeah. Which'd be fine if I thought it was what he really wanted," he said, his voice lower but closer, like he was just a few feet behind me now.

My hands stilled and I half turned. "Maybe it is."

He took another step closer. "And maybe it's not." He took the oily rag from me. "I don't think it is. I saw how he looked at me last night."

I swallowed hard. He was close enough that I could feel the heat from his body, and it was too close. Too heady and far too close. I took a step back and felt the shelf along the back wall press against my back.

"What are you scared of?" he asked me.

I couldn't speak. I swallowed again and shook my head. "I'm... not..."

He ignored my pathetic attempt at denying it. "I better go, or they'll come looking for me," he said. "Look"—he ran his hands through his hair—"Billy and I won't be back 'til late, so you've got all day to think about it."

I was almost too scared to ask. "Think about what?"

He stepped right in close and, leaning against me, pressed me into the shelf. His smell, his touch, the feel of him against me, the heat of his skin made it impossible to breathe.

Travis ran his nose along my ear and ever so gently, he ghosted his lips over mine. It was an almost-kiss. A heart-stopping, knee-buckling kind of almost-kiss.

He stepped back and smirked. "That."

And then he handed me the oily rag, turned and walked out.

My fucking knees almost gave out. I had to lean forward, resting my hands on my knees, to catch my breath like I'd just tried to race a horse to the fence like I did when I was a kid.

My heart was hammering and my hands were shaking. I was kind of pissed off, to be honest, that I'd let him affect me that way. That I'd let him say that to me, *do* that to me. That I'd let him get so under my skin when he'd been here just a week and I'd promised myself I wouldn't jeopardise my professionalism when it came to him.

And I *wanted* to be pissed off because it would feed my resolve to put a stop to this nonsense. I *would* be pissed off, I told myself, so when he gets back to the homestead that night, I could tell him no.

I just had to stop smiling first.

***

DISTRACTED.

Distracted was a good way to describe the rest of my day. George would probably use the word useless, and he'd probably be right.

That fucking smug Yank had me going in circles. It was

pitiful. *I* was pitiful. And I knew when Travis got back to the homestead, I'd tell him that his behaviour was inappropriate, unprofessional and just plain wrong.

However he *thought* I looked at him in the hall the other night was wrong.

So what if he was the first half-naked man I'd seen in almost two years? So what if he had a star tattoo—a symbol for gay men—and so what if he looked like he wanted to pounce on me. So what if he was gay?

So what if I was gay too? It didn't mean anything. Just because we were the only two gay men in a three hundred kilometre radius didn't mean squat.

Just because I dreamed of him, fantasised about him— just because I wanted him—didn't mean it could happen.

Because it couldn't.

And when Travis got back tonight, I'd tell him exactly that.

WE'D HAD dinner minus Travis and Billy, and I had been in my office for a few hours when I heard a familiar laugh outside. I closed my laptop and sighed.

Next, I heard Ma in the kitchen. "Boys are back," she called out.

Knowing what I had to do, I went outside. The sun had all but disappeared, the air had cooled and the horizon was a perfect Outback sunset mix of orange, pinks and purples. I walked over to where Billy and Travis were standing alongside their horses.

Billy said, "Got 'em all in, boss. Turned the water off in the top paddock and closed the gates."

"Thanks," I said, looking over the horses. They were

covered in red dirt and sweat. I presumed the two men weren't too much better. "You boys wanna go and cleaned up. Ma's reheating your dinner." I walked around to Billy's horse, not making eye contact with Travis.

"We'll clean the horses up first, hey, boss?" Billy asked.

"I'll do it," I said, taking both sets of reins and leading the horses toward the shed. I didn't wait for a reply, but when I tethered the horses and started to unsaddle them, I looked back and both men were gone.

Fuck.

I hosed the horses down, brushed them and then fed them with a knot in my stomach. I hated feeling like this. And when I couldn't put off going back inside any longer, Billy walked out. He rubbed his stomach. "Good tucker," he said.

I hung the last bridle up and smiled at him. I liked Billy. He was a bit rough, uneducated—I doubted he could read or write—but he was as genuine as they came. "Ma's tucker is always good."

"Travis did real good today, boss."

"Did he?" I asked quietly.

"Yeah. Funny fella too."

I felt a twinge of jealousy and sadness that it was something I wouldn't know firsthand. I was grateful it was dark so he couldn't see my expression. "Is he?"

Billy grinned, his white teeth looked whiter still against his dark skin and the darkening night behind him. "Was roundin' 'em up real good, goin' flat strap and his horse spooked. Almost came off."

"Was he alright?"

"He's fine," Billy said with a laugh. "All he could do was laugh, boss."

And there it was again. Jealousy and sadness. Though now it was mostly sadness.

"Can be on my team any day," Billy said. "Better hit the hay, hey, boss?"

I gave a nod. "You've got an easy day tomorrow."

"Sure thing," he said as he walked off, and when I was left standing there, I knew I had to go inside and face him.

I only got inside the front door. I could see the kitchen light was off, as was the dining room light, the lounge room was empty, so I figured he must have been in his room. I walked through the door off the foyer to where our bedrooms were and he was leaning against the hall wall just a few feet away, waiting for me.

I stopped dead, my stomach was knotted and my heart was in my throat. "Travis," I said just above a whisper.

He smiled. "Charlie," he said, all gruff and southern.

I swallowed hard and finally found my voice. "We can't..."

Travis frowned and nodded. "Fair enough." Then after a little while, he said, "So are you just gonna ignore me for the rest of my time here? Is that what you do? Just act like I'm not here? Because for the first two days I thought we got on real well, then... nothing. You won't even look at me."

My heart was thumping so damn loud I'm surprised he couldn't hear it. I opened my mouth to say something, but no words would come.

"So, this morning," he said. He took a step forward, still wearing his dirty jeans and shirt. His hair was all flat where he'd worn a hat all day. "Was I wrong? Because your mouth is saying no, but your eyes are saying yes."

I looked to the wall beside him. *Fuck.* I took a deep breath and shook my head.

He took another step forward and lifted his hand to

touch my shirt, my face, I didn't know. "What are you scared of?"

I grabbed his hand before he could touch me and pushed him against the hall wall, holding his hand above his head. My face was half an inch from his, looking up at him. His eyes were wide and dark.

"You," I snarled at him. "I'm scared of you."

And then I kissed him. Not a half-kiss, not a ghost-kiss, but I was rough. I covered my mouth with his and I kissed him for all I was worth.

He pulled his hand from where I had it pinned above his head, and I thought he would push me away. But he pulled my face closer, his fingers snaked around my neck and he kissed me back.

Our tongues touched and I groaned, my blood caught fire and I could feel the ache building in my belly.

Travis wrapped one arm around my waist, pulling at my shirt and then running his hands on my back. His skin on mine made me shiver and I pulled my mouth from his to breathe.

But he didn't stop. He kissed my jaw, down my neck, under my ear and I could feel him smile against my skin when I shivered again.

He looked at me then. For a long moment, his pale blue eyes were dark and his lips were swollen red. He pushed me backward through my bedroom door. And I should have stopped him, I should have said no.

But I fisted the front of his shirt and pulled him into my room with me.

His smile, even in the darkened room, was spectacular.

"Fucking smug Yank," I mumbled.

He laughed, a deep throaty chuckle, so I kissed him again to shut him up. I held his face as we kissed, our lips and tongues fused and his hands roamed my back, my sides and then he was fumbling with the fly on my jeans.

I pulled back from him to undo the buttons myself and he grinned and laughed again, so I pushed him back onto my bed. I crawled over him, both our jeans undone, and I rubbed my cock against his. Even through our briefs, I almost came at the feel of him underneath me.

It had been so long.

I kissed him again, devouring his mouth, sliding my tongue against his. With his hands on my arse, Travis pulled my hips into his and moaned into my mouth, "Fuck."

Then he did it again.

And again.

And I was thrusting, rubbing against him. Our hard cocks slid pushing, seeking friction, anything.

"Oh God," I groaned. "Fuck, I'm gonna come."

Gripping my arse, he pulled my hips into his harder, faster, and the room spun and my vision went white and painless fire ripped through my body as I came.

Travis bucked underneath me, groaning long and low, and there was a hot mess between us. I collapsed on top of him and he was writhing, and I realised he'd come too.

I rolled off him onto my back beside him. He chuckled. "Jesus," he said. "Man, I wanted to do that since the first day I got here."

I lifted my arm but it was too heavy and spongy and when it fell back down, it hit his chest, making him laugh. "Shut up," I told him, chuckling myself.

He rolled onto his side facing me. "You're something to see when you come."

I barked out a laugh, embarrassed at his candidness. "I, uh, I didn't see your face, sorry," I said, and then I cleared my throat. "I think I lost consciousness for a second."

He burst out laughing but tried to stifle it. "Gimme ten minutes and you can see it again if you like."

I chuckled and sighed. "We should probably get cleaned up."

"Lucky we do our own washing," he said. "God forbid if we had to explain jizz stains to Ma."

I laughed again, then tucked my dick back into my briefs. Travis, still on his side, made no attempt to hide himself. "Can I ask you something?" he asked.

"Oh. Um, I guess."

"How long since you last made out with someone?"

Even in the dark, I'm sure he could see me blush. "Why? Was I bad at it?"

He snorted. "Definitely not. Just curious. The boys said you don't go into the Alice on your weekends off. That they didn't know if you'd left this station in the two years since you've been back."

"Well," I said. I cleared my throat. "It's been a while."

"Two years?"

"Yeah, about that," I admitted quietly.

"Then you got three weeks with me," he said. "Before I leave. You better make the most of it."

I laughed and covered my face in my hands. "The staff don't know," I said, still hiding my face. "Well, George and Ma know I'm gay, but no one else. They can't know."

"Your call. But no one else *has* to know," he said simply. He peeled my hands from my face so I'd look at him. "But I don't want you to ignore me like you have these last few days," he said, serious now.

"Ignore you?" I pretended I didn't know what he was talking about.

"Yes. You don't need to fight it anymore. I think we're

past the *I wonder if he's interested* thing." When I didn't say anything, he added, "Two years, really?"

I snorted out a laugh. "Yeah, thanks for not bringing it up twice or anything."

He laughed this time. "It's just a really long time. How old are you?"

"Twenty-five."

"It's just a really long time for a twenty-five-year-old to go between drinks, if you know what I mean?"

"Not many single gay men come out this way."

He put his hand on my chest. "Well, I'm here now, so you may as well take advantage of the opportunity."

I frowned, dreading saying out loud the very reason I was afraid in the first place.

I took a deep breath and said, "Um, when we're working... during the day..."

"Charlie, I get it. During the day, we work. At night, we play."

I snorted at that. "So what am I? A working holiday conquest?"

He grinned that bloody smug smile, then leaned in and kissed me. It started soft and sweet, but then he cradled my face with his hand and he pulled himself over to me. Putting his hand on my stomach, he slid his hand under the elastic of my briefs and wrapped his fingers around my cock.

"We may as well only get cleaned up once," he whispered against my lips.

I ran my hands over his side, laughing when he squirmed. "Are you ticklish?" I asked.

He grabbed my hand and put it on his hardening dick. "Not here I'm not."

I palmed his cock and gripped him, making his tongue

stutter in my mouth. I smiled against his lips and he replied by cupping my balls and kissing me harder.

Lying on our sides, kissing, stroking, it was slower this time. More... intimate. I was soon thrusting into his hand, unable to help myself. Unable to stop the pressure building, unable to hold back.

The more I wanted release, the more I pumped him, and he was soon bucking into my hand. I stopped kissing him so I could watch him this time, and as his eyes closed, his mouth opened and his neck corded as he flexed into my fist. His cock swelled and spilled hot cum onto both of us.

Travis's whole body jerked, and swatting his hand away, I took my own cock in hand as my orgasm rocked through me. Travis was on me then, while I was coming, rolling onto me and thrusting his tongue in my mouth.

Our kisses became languid as our bodies simmered, and Travis eventually rolled off me, lay flat on his back and chuckled.

Then I started to laugh. "We're a bit of a mess."

"Shower?"

He leapt up, took my hand and pulled me off the bed. The house was quiet and God only knows if Ma and George heard what we'd just done. Part of me was horrified, and part of me didn't care. Travis got in the shower first; it wasn't hardly big enough for two. He scrubbed himself down, and I watched him be all wet and naked in the shower.

He had no other tattoos, just the star on his chest. He was lean but muscular and tanned, his uncut dick heavy and spent.

"Enjoying the view?" he asked.

"Sorry," I said. It was different now, being all out in the

open in a well-lit bathroom as opposed to a darkened bedroom.

He shut the water off and stepped out of the shower, dripping wet and smiling. "Don't go getting all shy now. You weren't shy ten minutes ago. Or half an hour ago in the hall, for that matter."

I chuckled a bit and looked at floor. "I'm not used to this," I said, waving my hand between us. "Are you always so forthright?"

He plucked his towel off the rack, and without an ounce of modesty, wiped his face and hair dry, still buck naked. "Uh, yeah."

I stripped out of my clothes, trying not to feel self-conscious by being naked in front of him, which was stupid, considering what we'd just done. I smiled at him and got into the shower, quickly washing myself. Water wasn't something we had in great supply, so showers were always short. By the time Travis had brushed his teeth at the basin, I was out and had the towel around my waist.

Travis was at least wearing his towel now, and a grin. "So? Third time's a charm?"

I scoffed. "Uh, I think sleep actually might be the charm." I opened the bathroom door and waited for him. "After you."

"Are you holding the door so you can check out my ass?"

I laughed. "No, I was just being polite."

"I'd rather you checked out my ass," he said as he walked to his bedroom door. He stopped. "My bed's awfully big and yours smells like sex, so if you wanna sleep in here with me..."

I turned the light off and walked to my bedroom door. "I think mine'll be fine."

Just as I was about to say goodnight, he spoke. "Charlie?"

"Yeah?"

He walked up the hall, and leaning in, he kissed me softly. "You don't have to be scared of me anymore." I tried to say something back to him, but he lifted my chin and kissed me again. "Goodnight."

I nodded. "Night."

I shut my door and got into bed. I was trying not to think about what he said, but he was right about one thing. My bed really smelled of sex. I rolled over and smiled into my pillow, and I slept like the dead.

I WOKE UP LATE, very unlike me, and met a smug, grinning Travis in the kitchen. Ma was there getting breakfast ready, oblivious to the look he was giving me.

"Sleep okay?" he asked with a knowing grin. "You look like you just woke up."

"I did just wake up," I said, my voice still croaky with sleep.

"Oh." Ma turned then. "You feel okay? I thought you were up and outside already."

"I'm fine," I said, taking a cup from the tray and pouring myself a tea.

Travis grinned behind Ma, but then he picked up the tray of tea and coffee and took it to the dining room, and I had a sense of dread that what we'd done last night was a mistake. I had told him explicitly that no one could know, and the very next morning he was all too-knowing-smiles and innuendos.

But when we were seated at the table, he never even

looked at me. It was like any other day. He laughed with Billy about their day in the top paddocks yesterday, retelling the stories of how he'd almost fallen off Texas, making everyone laugh as he did.

Even me.

He was playing his part perfectly. If scenes from last night weren't so fresh in my mind, if I didn't know how the hands he talked so animatedly with now felt on my skin, I'd wonder if it had happened at all.

When everyone had finished eating, George asked me, "What's the plan for today?"

I swallowed my last mouthful of food and sipped my tea. "Trudy and Fish head northwest, Bacon and Ernie northeast, open the gates and turn the water off. The cattle will come down on their own. Do a run for stragglers, herd them down. Go on the bikes, give the horses a rest." I didn't have to tell them to take their supply bags, walkie-talkies and a satellite phone. It was standard procedure. "Billy and Travis did their run yesterday. They can help out here."

George gave his usual nod, and as we all stood and headed out, he said, "Billy, Travis, you're with me."

Travis didn't bat an eyelid. Just took his hat off the hallstand, fixed it on his head and without so much as a backward glance, he jumped off the veranda as he followed George into the yard.

I had some paperwork to finalise on the ear tags, registering numbers. It was mostly done electronically these days, which saved time. We'd section off the yearlings, females and breeding stock and tag them accordingly, releasing them back into the paddocks. I spent the day running holding tape, making temporary fences in the southern paddocks, only hearing the occasional burst of laughter from the storage sheds.

Later that night when Travis and Billy were finishing up, George stood on the veranda with me. "How'd the boys go today?" I asked casually.

"Real good. That kid is a worker, ain't no two ways about it. Didn't even have to tell him to do, he just gets in and does it."

I nodded and bit the inside of my lip so I wouldn't smile. "Billy said he held his own yesterday. Normally a full ten-hour day up in those top paddocks will bring 'em home wrecked or crying. But he came back laughing."

George snorted out a laugh. "Is that why you paired him with Billy? Not many folk can keep up with him."

I smiled this time. "Maybe."

"Or was it to get rid of him for the day?"

I snorted and probably blushed a little. "Maybe."

George smiled, something he didn't do too often. "Anyways, he's worth his keep. Shame he can't stay on a bit longer, huh?"

I didn't answer that one.

George looked from me back out to Travis. His voice was quiet. "That's what I thought." He grinned at me, clapped me on the shoulder then yelled out for the two of them to get cleaned up for dinner.

TRAVIS ACTUALLY PLAYED his part so well, by the end of the day, I thought maybe he didn't want to do anything again. He didn't ignore me, but I kept waiting for some look of recognition or a hint of suggestion in a passing comment, but it never came. Apart from the grin and eyebrow waggle first thing this morning in the kitchen, he'd not even really looked at me.

It was exactly what I asked him to do. I couldn't fault

him for that. I just wondered if I was that easy to resist, to ignore. Was I really that forgettable?

Like every night, I spent a few hours after dinner in my office. I could hear Travis and George talking from where they sat on the veranda. George was trying to explain Australian Football, and it wasn't going well. Travis couldn't seem to get past the fact it was played on an oval-shaped field, and it would make me smile every time George had to re-explain something.

Then they started on cricket.

He had the patience of a saint, but in the end, George gave up and called it a night. I heard the front door open and close again, but the house was quiet and I presumed Travis had gone to bed too. As much as I wished it otherwise, I couldn't ignore the lump of disappointment in my belly.

I stared at my office for a while, lost in my head, and I didn't hear the door open. "Are you avoiding me?" Travis asked quietly. He was leaning against the doorframe, his bare feet framed by his jeans and blue-and-white-checkered shirt. The sleeves were rolled to his elbows. He startled me, and smiled when I put my hand to my heart.

"I thought you were avoiding me," I replied.

His eyes flickered with confusion. "You told me to."

"I know I did." I shook my head at how stupid I sounded. "Sorry."

Travis smiled warmly and walked into my office. He leaned his ass on the side of my desk like he owned it. "So if you're not avoiding me..."

I closed my laptop and stood up, not really wanting to have this conversation anywhere besides the privacy of my room. I went to walk past him. "I'm not avoiding you. I just don't think here is the best—"

His hand on my arm stopped me. "Everyone's gone to bed," he whispered. He was still leaning against my desk and he pulled me toward him and smiled. "Ever had desk sex?"

"Travis," I hissed at him. "Not here."

He frowned and looked down at the desk over his shoulder. "We could try carrying it into your room, but it looks heavy."

I laughed, despite trying not to. "That's not what I meant."

He grinned. "I know." Then he stood up, and with his hand still on my arm, he leaned in close. His body heat, his smell made my head swim. He ran his nose along my ear, making me shiver, then nudged his nose against mine in an almost-kiss. "I'm going to bed. I think you should come with me."

He walked out, and I had to adjust myself before I followed him. I turned off the lights, closed the front door, and by the time I got to my bedroom door, I wondered if he meant my bed or his. I hesitated, which he must have heard, because there was a chuckle from my room.

"Shut up," I said, walking in and closing the door behind me. "I didn't know which room you went into."

The room was dark, my eyes not yet adjusted to the lack of light. He laughed again but then his hands were on the button of my jeans. I ran my hands up his arms and over his naked chest and back, over his ass. He was only wearing briefs. Then I did something I'd wanted to do all damn day.

I kissed him.

Hard.

I held his head in both hands and kept his mouth pressed to mine. I fed him my tongue and his hands stopped on my jeans, falling to his sides, and he melted into me, totally owned by this kiss.

When I finally slowed and pulled my mouth from his, he groaned. "Goddamn," he said breathily. "Fuck... kiss me... like that..."

I'd rendered him speechless. I chuckled and kissed him again, softer this time. He went back to undressing me.

I pulled his underpants down, releasing his cock, feeling it spring against me. He shoved my jeans and briefs down over my hips and I stepped on them, trying to get out of them without using my hands. I didn't want to stop touching him. I wanted to feel him everywhere.

Travis slid his hand around my cock. "You didn't answer my question about desk sex," he whispered in my ear.

I laughed against his neck, kissing down his collarbone. "Get on the bed."

He was quick to obey and I crawled up over him. He had his hand on his own dick, and I swatted it away, licking him instead. I was rewarded almost immediately with precum, making me groan.

His whole body jerked and he moaned loudly. I smiled and slid my lips over the head of his cock, swirling my tongue and sucking. It had been a long time since I'd given head—and I'd forgotten just how much I loved doing it.

Travis squirmed underneath me, then pulled me off him. "Stop."

"What's wrong?"

"Get up here," he said, his voice gruff. "Turn around. I want to taste you too."

He sat up on the bed, took my face in his hands and pulled me in for a quick kiss, then lay back down diagonally on the bed. He put his hand on my hip and urged me to face the other way. Leaning into position, I swung my leg over his chest and gave him what he wanted.

He took me into his mouth as I did the same to him. It took every ounce of control not to fuck his mouth but to keep my hips still and let him move as he wanted. I worked him over, and as we gave mutual blowjobs, mutual pleasure, it wasn't long until I was close to coming.

I pulled my mouth off his cock to warn him, but he took hold of my hips and slid me in deeper as I came down his throat.

Still riding my orgasm high, I somehow managed to remember to keep sucking and pumping him until he arched under me. "God, gonna come," he warned, and I wanted it. I wanted to taste him, drink him, so I slid my fingers over his balls, and he bucked, filling my mouth with cum, and I swallowed hungrily.

I rolled off him, collapsing at his side. I wanted to kiss him but was facing the wrong way, so I leaned over and kissed his thigh instead. Travis chuckled and convulsed as an aftershock wracked through him. He tried to pull my arm. "Get up here," he mumbled.

I shuffled up so I was lying the same way as him with my head on a pillow. Travis lifted my arm off my chest and nestled himself into my side, using my chest as a pillow. My arm fell comfortably around his shoulder, holding him. Without realising what I was doing, I pressed my lips to his forehead. He leaned up and kissed my lips softly, then put his head back down and draped his arm over me.

It was an intimate thing to do. It was unexpected but comforting. And really fucking wonderful.

I had every intention of telling him he couldn't sleep in my bed, but before I knew it, it was morning.

And I was alone.

THE NEXT TWO days were the same. All work during the day—never once giving anything away—and all playful and fucking sexy as hell at night.

He fell asleep in my bed each night, waking up sometime earlier than me to go back to his room. I never asked him why; I presumed it part of the discretion clause I'd put in earlier.

We hadn't had intercourse. We'd done just about everything else, but there'd been no penetrative sex. I'd had my finger in his ass, but nothing else. I wanted to, I wanted to be inside him so bad, and I was going to ask him if it was something he'd consider.

Some guys didn't like it, and that was fair enough. Throughout my few years at college, I preferred to top. Maybe that was more to do with my impatience and need to fuck as much as I could. That said, some of the best sex I'd had was when I bottomed. With the right person, a patient and attentive person, it could take you to places of pleasure you never knew existed.

And if all I had for the rest of my life was a few short weeks of sex and fun, then I wanted to do it all. But only if Travis wanted that too. I didn't even know if he topped or bottomed. I had a feeling if it came down to specifics, I wouldn't care.

It was late on Friday night when I got a call from my closest neighbour. Greg Pietersen had run Burrunyarrip Station for as long as I could remember. He'd helped me out when my dad passed away, driving the two-hundred-and-fifty-kilometre trip across the Queensland border to come over.

It was mustering time across the Outback, and all

stations kept in touch so we knew what the other was up to. Sometimes we borrowed staff or equipment, sometimes we lent it out. This was one of those times.

Greg's helicopter, same as ours, was out of action. The part would take a week to get in, but they were rounding up these next two days, and even with such short notice, he wanted to know if I'd help.

"Of course," I said into the phone without hesitating. "I can come over and help out tomorrow."

George stood in the doorway and heard enough of the conversation. He was probably already getting things organised in his head for me to head out the next morning, gave a nod and waved goodnight.

About ten minutes later, while Greg and I discussed details and GPS locations, Travis came into my office. He pulled the door closed behind him and his lips were twisted in an attempt not to smile, but his eyes were full of spark.

I put my hand over the receiver and whispered, "What are you doing?"

He just grinned and walked around to my side of my desk, and while Greg talked in my ear, Travis slowly bent over my desk. He gripped the far side of the desk and slowly rocked his ass back and forth.

Jesus fucking Christ.

My balls ached at the sight alone, and my dick started to fill. I guess that answered my question about whether he topped or bottomed.

I wrapped up my call to Greg, not really hearing anything he'd said after that, but I told him I'd call in the morning to see if anything had changed. My voice was pitchy, and Travis smiled.

I put the phone down. "What do you think you're doing?"

"You never answered me the other night," he said, rocking his hips again. "About the desk sex."

I had to palm my dick. "Never on a desk, no."

"That's a shame," he said simply. He leaned up slowly, sticking his ass out. "What about the normal, boring, bed sex?"

I stood up behind him and pressed myself against his ass, suppressing a groan. I leaned over him. "Plenty," I whispered in his ear. "But it was never boring."

He moaned out a laugh, but then I remembered something. I let my forehead rest on the back of his neck and sighed. "I don't have any condoms," I whispered. "Sorry. I wasn't expecting to need any, and it's been a long time..."

Travis didn't even turn around and look at me. He just grabbed my hand and led me out of the office. I managed to hit the light switch on my way past and then close the front door as we went through the foyer to the hall. He stopped at my bedroom and let go of my hand. "Wait here."

He kept walking to his room while I stood there, not sure what the hell was going on. I opened my bedroom door and took a slow step inside. I was still hard, and I was nervous. Travis walked in behind me and threw a box of condoms and small bottle of lubricant on my bed. "I have some," he said, shutting the door behind him.

The room was dark, I couldn't see him, but my body seemed to know exactly where he was. He put his hand on my arm; finding me in the dark, he trailed his hands up to my neck and he kissed me. Still kissing, with roaming hands pulling at each other's clothes, we undressed and when finally naked, Travis turned around in my arms.

With my cock pressed against the crack of his ass, he leaned back into me and moaned. I kissed his shoulder and ran my hands all over his chest, his stomach, and finally wrapped my fingers around his rigid cock.

He stepped forward, holding my hands to keep me close behind him, then knelt on my bed. He leant forward so he was on his hands and knees, and then slowly, he laid down, lifting his ass and sliding a hand underneath him, stroking, waiting. I was transfixed, staring at his body before me, silver in the lightless room.

"Charlie," he hissed.

I crawled over him, kissing up his back before nipping the back of his neck. "You're a pushy bottom, huh?"

He turned his face. "I'll be a pushy top if you don't hurry up."

I laughed quietly and sat back, straddling his thighs. I rolled a condom down my cock, biting back a groan at the touch, then grabbed the bottle of lube. I slicked my fingers, then let a few drops run down his crack to his hole. I slid one finger into him, then two, and by the time he was ready for me, he was pushing back onto my hand and I was so turned on I could barely stand it. "I won't last long," I told him.

He answered with a groan and his right arm moved faster as he worked his own cock. "God, just do it."

I gave my balls a tug, trying to dampen the sensation in hopes I didn't come before I was inside him. I pressed my cock at his hole and, leaning forward over him, rolled my hips, pushing inside.

Ho. Ly. Fuck.

He groaned long and low as I slid into him, and my pleasure was forgotten in fear that I'd hurt him. I stilled. "You okay?"

Travis pressed his forehead into the mattress and moaned. His thighs were still spread, his hips were still off the bed, and he never stopped jerking himself off. "Keep going," he ground out.

I rubbed his back, his hips and thighs as I pushed all the way inside him. When I could go no farther, he let go of his cock to reach up above his head and grip the sheets instead. I reached around and took his cock in my hand, stroking him, and it was only then that I started to move.

I thrust into his ass in time with my hand, long, hard, deep, wanting to make it good for him. I focused on his needs first. I lifted his hips so he was on his knees, which gave me more room. I ran my other hand over his back, then around his front, and reaching down, I cupped his balls, using my forearms to pull him back onto me.

All I could do was roll my hips, making each turn short and sharp. I was so far inside him. He was hot and tight around me, and the coil of pleasure in my belly was wound tight.

Then I couldn't stop it. I stroked him faster and fucked him harder, and he bucked back onto me once, twice, three times, and he came. His back arched and his head fell forward as his orgasm rocketed through him. All I could do was hang on. And as he twitched and groaned, I drove into him over and over. The room spun, and god knows what sounds I made; my blood caught fire and I came.

I collapsed on top of him, slowly pulling out of him but not getting off him, and he chuckled. "Jesus Christ, Charlie."

"Hm mm."

He laughed again. It was warm and throaty and rumbled under me. "We need to get cleaned up. Me and these sheets are a mess," he said.

"Shame," I mumbled. "I liked how they smelled of you."

He chuckled again and hummed.

Realising I probably shouldn't have said that out loud, I pried myself off him and rolled onto the bed. "Want me to get a washcloth and wipe you down? Or do you want a shower?"

"You can do both," he said. My eyes had adjusted to the dark and he was smiling, but he looked sleepy.

He looked fucking sexy as hell.

He held out his hand, which I took without thinking. After a few seconds, he chuckled. "Well, I thought you might help me up, but you can hold my hand if you want."

I dropped his hand, grateful he couldn't see me blush. So then I tickled him. He shot up laughing, and only then did I grab his hand and pull him off the bed. "Oh, shit!" I said a little too late. "Are you sore? I shouldn't have made you jump like that."

"I'm fine," he replied. "Really, I am. But I have dried cum all over me." He waved his hand over his stomach and chest. "So, unless you're gonna wash it or lick it off me..."

I laughed and led the way down the darkened hall to the bathroom.

I WAS up at my normal time before Travis, and I worried that he might be sore. When we had a moment of privacy, I asked him again if he felt okay.

"I feel great actually," he said with that damn spark in his eye. "Though, just to be sure, maybe you should do it again. You know, just to be completely sure."

I rolled my eyes but couldn't stop from smiling. I'm pretty sure Ma thought something was up—she'd eyed me funny a few times over the last few days, as though I had a neon flashing light above my head that read, "Yes, I finally got laid."

If George knew, he certainly didn't let on. At breakfast, he brought up the telephone conversation from last night. "Headin' over to Burrunyarrip?"

Everyone at the table looked at me, waiting for me to answer. "Yeah. I spoke to Greg first thing this morning," I said. "He doesn't need a team or anything. Just that his chopper is down and needs mine for today, that's all. Said I'd do it for him."

George nodded. "She's fuelled and ready."

"Thanks."

George looked at everyone and gave orders for the day. It'd be a day around the homestead; there was always plenty to do.

As everyone stood up to leave, I sipped my tea and put my cup on the table. "Travis. You're with me."

CHAPTER SEVEN

THE WEIGHT OF WORDS AND DEMONS. THEY WEREN'T HEAVY UNTIL HE WENT AND POINTED 'EM OUT.

"SEE THAT FENCE DOWN THERE?" I asked, pointing down to the ground as we flew over. Travis could hear me through the headset.

He nodded. "Yeah?"

"That's the famous rabbit-proof fence. It means you just crossed state lines. We're now in Queensland."

I took us to the GPS coordinates Greg had given me, and it wasn't long before a group of men on horses and dirt bikes came into view. I took the chopper down and was met by Greg and a few of his staff. They looked at the stranger I'd brought with me.

I don't know why I was surprised. I just presumed he'd have stayed back, maybe even behind me, but of course he didn't. He walked right along with me, and after I shook Greg's hand and before I could introduce him, Travis held out his hand and introduced himself. "Travis Craig."

He wasn't smug or in your face, he was just really genuine. He'd smile warmly and give them his undivided attention. And he was confident. He wasn't shy—in any aspect—and he had a jump-in-with-both-feet kind of attitude.

I liked it.

I envied it.

With Greg's orders, Travis and I got back into the helicopter. I waited for the two on horseback to get a fair distance before taking her up. It wasn't long before we'd reached the top of the paddock, and I swung it back around and took her low to the ground. Maybe two metres from the dirt below us, I edged a small herd of Hereford closer.

At first, Travis's eyes were wide and his grin even wider as we brought in cattle from the far ends of the property. I remember the first time I ever went mustering by helicopter, and it was hard not to smile at him. But it wasn't long before he was navigating, pointing out any cattle he could see off in the distance. We made a pretty good team.

We spent a good few hours mustering, rounding up cattle and helping out. We refuelled at Greg's station, had lunch with him and his men and I called George to let him know we were done.

It was common courtesy and good safe practice in the Outback to always let someone know where you were going and if you were going to be late.

"Not coming straight home. We're headed up the north-east corner," I told George. "We'll be home for dinner though."

"No worries," George replied.

I hung up the receiver and put my headset on. I started the chopper, waved a goodbye to Greg and the boys and lifted us off the ground.

"Where we goin'?" Travis asked. "What's at the north-east corner?"

I grinned at him. "Thought we could go for a swim."

His whole face lit up, and then his eyes went wide. "Are there crocodiles?"

I laughed. "Nah. Not where we're going."

He seemed to relax a little but eyed me every so often as though he didn't believe me. I showed him the scenery as we went, pointing out landmarks and the ridge that ran along the eastern line of my property. I explained it was about fifteen kilometres from the homestead and was about twenty kilometres long and was the only real provision of shade in the afternoon sun. Travis was fascinated in the layered limestone, and I told him I'd take him in for a closer look.

I kind of forgot he was here to study.

I pointed out our destination and pulled the helicopter down in a clearing. It was a bit of a climb up through the rocky ridge outcrop. It was a secluded watering hole, fed by a natural spring, with the wall of the ridge on one side casting an afternoon shadow over half the pool. The water was clear, cool and waist deep.

Travis grinned. "How the hell did you ever find this place?" he asked. "It's like your own oasis!"

"Cattle. They found it, I followed them. But we closed off this paddock after bringing the cattle down about a month ago."

"Is this where you come swimming?" he asked. "When we got back from the Alice, you'd been swimming."

"Yep."

He pulled his shirt over his head and tossed it, then pulled his boots off and stopped to stare at me. "And no crocodiles."

"None. Could be snakes though," I told him seriously. I pulled my shirt over my head and toed out of my boots. He hadn't moved. "If one comes by, just stay real still."

"Just stay real still?" he repeated. "Jesus. How many deadly snakes are there out here?"

I laughed. "You're probably better off not knowing." I took off my jeans and pulled off my socks, then walked out into the water wearing only my briefs. I could see the bottom easily, so I dived in feeling the cool water soothe my heated skin.

When I came up, I turned around to see Travis walking in. He was wearing his briefs as well, and as soon as the water was to his thighs, he dived in and joined me. "God, this is good," he said when he came up.

"It's perfect, isn't it? Hard to imagine swimming holes being out here."

He floated on his back, fully relaxing on the surface of the water, and for a long while we just enjoyed the cool water and the absolute silence of the Outback. It was comfortable between us, no awkward silences and no awkward attempts at conversation.

When our skin was starting to prune, we got out and sat on the large sheets of rock in the shade. Travis lay back and sighed. "How is this the northeast corner?" he asked. "If your land goes for hundreds of kilometres and we're only, what? Thirty kilometres from the homestead?"

"Northeast corner of the first eastern paddock," I explained. "George knows what I'm talking about."

Travis snorted. "This place is really fucking big, isn't it?"

I laughed and lay back on the rock, the warmth of it seeping into my back. "Yeah, it's pretty big. Australia's about the same size of America, yeah?"

"Yeah."

"Just that you got fifty states, and we've got seven."

"It's amazing though," he said. He pointed up to the

wall of the ridgeline. "Look at that. The lines in the limestone and sediment faults. This place has been wearing down in the wind and rain for millions of years."

"You really love it, don't you?" I asked, looking over at him and smiling. "The geology and soil sciences of it all."

"I wouldn't say I *love* it," he countered. "I understand it, and I appreciate it. And... okay, so maybe I do love it a little bit."

I snorted and we were quiet again for another short while.

Then out of nowhere, he said, "Next time we come here, we're bringing condoms. We could have sex in the sun."

"In the shade," I corrected. "Don't think you'd fancy getting your dick sunburned."

He laughed and for a long moment, he lay in warm shade with his eyes closed.

"Did you buy those condoms in Sydney? It's not really my business, I'm just curious, that's all."

He opened one eye, looked at me with it, then smiled. "Yes."

I shrugged. "It doesn't matter to me," I lied. "I just wondered, that's all."

"It was a twelve pack," he said, still with his eyes closed. "I used two in Sydney."

"Oh."

He rolled onto his side, resting his head on his hand and smirked. "Sounds like a jealous *oh*."

I barked out a laugh. "A twelve pack was ambitious, yes?"

He laughed. "You *are* jealous!"

"No I'm not," I shot back, quickly sitting up.

He jumped up and grabbing my hands, he pulled me to

my feet, then kissed me with smiling lips. "Green looks good on you."

I pushed him and he laughed, running back into the water.

We swam again for a while, then floated on our backs, which led to splashing, which led to wrestling in the water, which led to making out in the water, which led to more making out on the rocks in the shade.

I was on my back and he was on top of me. His kisses got slower, he pulled my lips between his and, still with his eyes closed, did that nose-nudge thing that made my brain stutter. Then he pulled away completely and lay down beside me. He sighed loudly, closed his eyes and licked his lips.

I closed my eyes too and just enjoyed being there in my sacred place with him. I never thought I'd ever, ever bring someone here. Let alone a man.

"Tell me about you," he said casually. "What's the Charlie Sutton story?"

I turned my head to look at him. He'd been watching me. "Well," I started. "I um," I let out a nervous breath.

"You don't have to tell me if you don't want."

And I didn't really want to. I hadn't thought of that shit in years, but there was something about him, something about the way he looked at me, something that made me tell him.

"My mum left when I was four," I said, looking back up at the sky. He didn't say anything to that, just listened. "I remember she had brown hair and a green dress. But that's it, that's all I remember of her. I guess she got sick of the desert. Got sick of the red dirt." I'd never told anyone that. I looked out over the offending scenery. "It was just me and Dad after then. And George and Ma. I probably spent more time with them than I ever did with my dad. He was busy running the station, I guess." I shrugged again.

"You went to school?"

"School of the Air out here," I explained. "Too remote for classrooms. I'd sit and have lessons over the two-way radio, and Ma'd help me with reading and writing when I was little."

"But you went to college?"

I smiled. "I did. I somehow graduated high school and went to Sydney." I shook my head. "Man, I was like a kid in a candy shop," I said with a laugh. Then I sighed. "My dad made me go. We didn't exactly get on. We weren't exactly close. Drove him mad enough, despite being a pair of hands he didn't have to pay wages to, that he insisted I go. In the end I think he was glad to get me out of his hair."

He studied me for a long while. "You didn't finish your degree," he said. It wasn't a question.

I shook my head again. "No. My dad was sick but never told anyone, apparently. Then it was too late. I got a phone call from George telling me he was real sick, and by the time I got home, he was gone."

Travis sat up then and frowned. "Shit. Did you speak to him when you were at college?"

"Yeah, it was okay. I mean, it was never going to be..." I started to explain then stopped. "I came home over Christmas breaks when I was in Sydney," I said with a sad smile. "Dad wasn't exactly an emotional man, but we were... okay."

"Did he know you... you know, liked boys?"

I snorted. "Uh, yeah."

Travis was quiet and he seemed awfully interested in his hands. "He didn't take it too well?"

"Not exactly." I imitated my father's voice. "*It'll be over my dead body that a fairy runs this station. It takes a man's man to survive out here.*" I couldn't believe I'd just said those words out loud. To someone else. I shook my head and sighed.

"Jesus," he whispered. "I'm sorry."

I tried smiling at him. "Those weren't the *last* words my father ever said to me."

"But he said them?"

I nodded. "Right before he packed me up and shipped me off to Sydney."

"And you were never close after that?"

"Or before it." I scoffed. "When I turned eighteen, the boys took me into Alice Springs, you know, thinkin' they'd get me drunk and get me laid. Well, that's exactly what happened, but probably just not the way they thought." My smile faded. "But then George caught me in the bathroom stalls of some bar with some guy. When we got back here, my old man knew something was up. George never said anything to him, but I had guilt written all over me and decided, in some foolish, wishful-thinkin' moment, that he might be okay with it."

Travis just listened, not saying a word, not taking his eyes off me.

"But having your one and only son, the heir to your well-respected station, as a faggot wasn't on my father's wish list apparently," I said, not even trying to hide the bitter taste to those words. "Hell, it wasn't even on his toleratin' list."

I exhaled loudly. "He packed me up and sent me to Sydney, enrolled me in college and told me I had four years to get it out of my system. Then I could come back and help him run the station, find a woman, get married, have kids and be a son he could be proud of." I smiled sadly at him.

"At least he never had to live through such a disappointment."

"Sorry, I didn't mean to pry," Travis said quietly. "And you're no disappointment, Charlie. Far from it. I bet if your father could see how you run this place, he'd be proud."

"Well, I doubt that, but thanks."

Travis opened his mouth and closed it a few times, obviously not sure what to say. I don't know why I unloaded all that on him. I'd never told anyone what I'd just told him, and I was kinda mad at myself for doing it.

Then breaking a long silence, he said, "You know there's nothing wrong with being gay?"

"I know that," I answered quickly with more anger than I should have.

I could feel his gaze burning into me and after a long while, he said, "Do you?"

I looked at him then, questioningly.

His eyes fell to his hands. It was the first time I'd ever seen him unsure. "It makes sense now."

"What does?"

He took a little while to answer. "I wondered what demons lurked in those eyes of yours. And that's what it is. You carry your father's words around with you." He stared at me with something I couldn't quite place. "I can't imagine the weight of them."

I tried to say something, but if he was aiming for a hard truth, his words hit their mark.

He must have taken my silence for a reason to keep talking. "I'm sorry he said that to you. I'm sorry he didn't understand. I'm sorry you've carried that for so long."

"I can't change who I am," I said with a shrug. "I know that. I tried. But I also can't be who I really am. I can't run Sutton Station as Charlie Sutton, the gay farmer."

"Why not?"

I barked out a humourless laugh. "My father was right about one thing. You can't have no fairy faggots runnin' farms. Not out here." I looked across the flat red landscape. "Men out here don't deal with men like that."

Travis sat up and pointed his finger at me. "That's bull-shit," he spat out; his anger was surprising. "Bull. Shit. I've got news for you, Charlie, but they've been dealing with a gay man for years, and they respect you. They admire you. Like your neighbour Greg, he was so grateful for you today."

"They respect me because I'm my father's son, and they admire me for coming back and not walking away when others would have. *Should* have. But if they knew—"

"If they knew, what difference would it make?" he said. "You'd still drop everything to go and help them. You'd still offer your time when you didn't have it to give, like today. Jesus, Charlie, give people like Greg some credit. What you do in your bedroom and what he does in his ain't nobody's business."

"You don't think I know that?" I asked.

He looked up to the sky and sighed. "I just hate seeing you completely resigned to being miserable for the rest of your life."

"Who said I'm miserable?"

Travis looked at me, daring me to argue, then he shrugged. The fight in him was gone. "Well, you're not miserable now, because I'm here."

I snorted. "Is that right?"

"Yeah, of course." He was quiet for a moment, and then he sighed loudly. "I don't mean to argue with you, and I don't want to make you feel bad. I'm not criticising or judging you."

I raised an eyebrow to differ.

He shook his head. "Really, I'm not. I know it can't be easy. Actually, I can't even imagine how hard it is. But I just wish... I wish they could see you the way I do."

I swallowed the lump in my throat. "What?"

"The Charlie that you are around me. The one that laughs and tells really bad jokes. The Charlie who's carefree and happy and who's really smart and kind. How you are around me."

"I'm not any different really," I mumbled quietly, knowing it was a lie.

Travis's eyes went wide. "Some people who've worked with you for two years have never heard you laugh!"

"That's staff, and that's different."

"I'm on your staff, and I was here for one day and you were laughing with me."

"I was laughing *at* you. That's the difference."

His mouth fell open, and I shot up and into the water. He ran after me and jumped on my back, pushing us both into the waist-deep water. I came up for air resting on my knees but Travis, keeping hold of my neck, swung himself around and straddled my hips. I wrapped my arms around him. Water dripped from his hair, his eyes were bright and he kissed me with wet, smiling lips. "I'm different to you and you know it."

"Are you always so..."

"Right?"

"I was going to say smug."

He kissed me again, slower and deeper this time. "Tell me I'm right."

I leaned in to kiss him instead of answering, but he pulled his face back. "Tell me I'm right."

"You're right," I told him.

He laughed and shook his head. "No, say I'm right about being different to you."

My smile died and my heart rate spiked at having to speak this truth out loud. "You're right," I admitted before I lost my nerve. Right there, in the cool blue water and the red ochre rocks, I told him, "I'm different around you. I can be me around you. From the second I saw you sitting in Ma's kitchen, I knew I was in trouble."

He leaned in and softly pressed his lips to mine. Then like it wasn't enough—like it would never be enough—he deepened the kiss. He kissed me like he *needed* it, like I was air and he was drowning. I could taste emotion on his tongue and feel it in the way he clung to me.

I carried him until the water shallowed and gently laid him down, pressing him into the sand as I lay on top of him. The water barely covered him, lapping over his skin, ebbing and flowing in time with our bodies.

Our kisses were slow and warm, with gentle lip bites and his signature nose-nudges that gave me butterflies.

"What's so funny?" he asked, kissing down my neck.

I hadn't realised I was smiling. "The way you do this," I said, softly nudging his nose with mine.

He rolled us over so I was in the water. I opened my legs for him and he settled his weight on me, then rolled his hips into mine. "I happen to like kissing you," he said gruffly. "And that's going to include these," he said, nudging my nose again.

"I happen to like it when you do that," I told him.

He bit his lip and stared into my eyes for a long, heart-thudding moment. "We probably should get going," he said finally, almost a whisper. "If we jizz in here, you might get funky-looking frogs."

I burst out laughing, and Travis knelt up off me,

palming his hard-on through his undies. He looked down at me, then at my crotch. "But if you want to stay..." He licked his lips.

I gave my dick a squeeze and hissed. "You can explain to Ma why we're late for dinner."

He leapt to his feet, grinning spectacularly, and held out to his hand to help me up. "Come on. Dinner first, you making me come three times later."

"Three times?"

"Too much? Not enough?"

I just shook my head. "Both."

DINNER CONSISTED of Travis using his hands and recounting our helicopter mustering day to the entire table, making people laugh the way he usually did.

I spent an hour or two after dinner with George going over the chopper while Travis looked on. We refuelled and cleaned her down and filled in the logbook, and when we were done, George called it a day. When we went back inside, seeing the house was dark and quiet, I'd barely got my hat on the rack when Travis pulled me into the hall and grinned at me.

"Up for round one?"

He didn't even give me time to answer. His mouth was on mine and he pushed me backward into my room, shutting the door behind us with his foot. He pulled my shirt over my head and he was urgent, passionate. Desperate.

I pulled away from him, needing air and a minute to make sense of the jumbled mess of thoughts in my head.

He undid his jeans and squeezed his dick. "Charlie," he whispered. "I've been on edge all damn day."

God, he *was* desperate. I kissed him softly and sweetly, setting the pace where I wanted it. Where I could make him feel so damn good.

I pushed him onto the bed. He fell on his back and I gripped the legs of jeans and pulled them off him. He took his own shirt off and then his briefs as I undressed myself.

"I put the box of rubbers in your drawer," he said, scooting up on the bed. He took his dick in one hand, and after bringing one foot up to his ass, he found his hole with his other hand and he slipped one finger in.

"Please, Charlie."

I grabbed a condom and the bottle of lube and threw them onto the bed beside him. He was working himself over, and it was turning me on just watching him. I'd never seen anything so hot.

I knelt between his legs, rolled the latex sheath down my cock, smeared lube on my hand and took over. "Let me."

"I shouldn't have stopped us at the lagoon," he said, bucking his hips. "I'm so fucking horny."

I smiled and slipped his cock into my mouth. He groaned and flexed under me and it was then I slipped my finger in his ass.

"Oh Jesus," he moaned, gripping the sheets beside him.

I sucked his cock and finger-fucked his ass until he was writhing and begging and finally coming in my mouth.

I drank down everything he gave me, and while he was still convulsing with waves of pleasure, I pushed his legs up to his chest and sunk my cock inside his arse.

His eyes went wide and his mouth fell open in a silent scream. I leaned over him, planting my mouth over his, letting him taste himself in my mouth. He was trembling and made a high-pitched whimpering sound in his throat that I'd never heard before. I thought it might have been too much for him, too much sensation, too much pleasure, but he clung to me. His arms were around my neck and his feet locked behind my back, keeping me there, and I oh so slowly thrust every inch into his arse.

I wanted to draw out every fibre of pleasure he had in him; I wanted him to come again.

I pulled my mouth from his to lean back a little. His lips were red and swollen and his eyes were still wide. Resting on one elbow, I slipped my other hand between us and took his cock in hand.

He shook his head quickly, *no no, no*, like it was all too much.

"I want you to come again," I told him, still jerking him off.

He grabbed my face and pulled our mouths back together, his tongue invading my mouth, and he tightened his legs around me. "Oh fuck," he whispered into my mouth.

I continued to work his cock between us as I rocked into him, as slowly and as deeply as I could. Then he cradled my face so he could stare into my eyes. It was intimate and beautiful, and a whole lot like making love.

My hand stopped, my eyes closed and my head fell down, not wanting to see that look in his eyes.

But he pulled my face up. "Look at me," he whispered. Then he rocked his hips, urging me to keep moving. I pushed in again and again, making him gasp with each thrust, and his eyes got wider and he lifted his hips and he started to shake and tremble. His cock swelled in my hand and he arched under me, crying out as he came again.

I let go of his cock so I could grip him under the shoulders, and I slammed into him. His whole body convulsed and jerked, and he groaned louder and louder.

I covered his mouth with mine to keep him quiet and as soon as my tongue filled his mouth, I came.

He clung to me as my orgasm swept through me, and when the room and my head stopped spinning, I pulled out of him and rolled us over. He whimpered and it was then I noticed he was still all twitchy and his hands were shaking.

Instinctively, I pulled him against me and wrapped my arms around him. "Jesus, are you okay?"

He laughed. It sounded a little maniacal. "Oh. Oh fuck."

I pulled back to look in his eyes and put my hand to his face, his forehead. "Travis?"

He opened his eyes and they were swimming; he looked drunk. "I've never..." he said drowsily. "What the fuck did you do to me?"

He was smiling and all pliable, still a little shaky, obviously more than fine. I pulled him back against me. "I think I found your prostate."

"Twice," he said with a laugh. A shiver ran through him and he twitched again. He snuggled into me, tucking his hands to our chests, and I tightened my arms around him. He chuckled again. "Fuck. I'm still shaking."

I pulled the sheet up over us and kissed the side of his head. "Do you feel okay?"

"I feel so fucking good right now," he murmured. "So good."

I smiled into the darkness. I ran my hands over his back and he was so quiet, so still, I thought he'd fallen asleep.

Then he pressed his lips to my chest. "I had the best day today."

I smiled and closed my eyes. It *had* been a great day. One of the best, if I was truly honest. It was a hot night, the ceiling fan not making a lick of difference to the air in room.

And as hot as it was with him in my arms, I didn't want to move.

And when I woke in the morning, he was still in my bed. He was on his stomach, his head turned to face the wall and the sheet down to his waist. I marvelled at the lines of his back, that so-soft hair at the nape of his neck, and the curve of his ass under the sheet.

My bed smelled of him, I smelled of him, and even though I knew he shouldn't spend the night in my bed—it was too high a risk of being caught—I didn't care.

The sight of him in my bed, sound asleep with sex-sleep-tousled hair, was something I'd never forget. I took in everything: every line, every muscle, the way the colours changed on his skin as the room grew lighter, and I burned it into memory.

I wanted to be able to recall, with perfect clarity, everything about this moment in five, ten or fifty years. Because I knew once he left, once he went back home to the States, I'd never have this again.

TRAVIS WAS HAVING a Skype conversation with his mum. It was on my laptop, which I'd happily handed over when he said it was his mother's birthday. From the kitchen, I could hear him telling her how much he was enjoying it. I didn't think twice about it, I made him a coffee, walked into the lounge room, handed it to him and sat down beside him.

"Mum, this is Charlie," Travis said.

That was when I looked at the screen and saw a woman's smiling face on it.

"Shit," I mumbled and stood up, careful not to spill my

cup of tea. I didn't realise it was a video call; I thought he just meant a Skype voice call.

Travis grabbed my hand and pulled me back down to the lounge. "He's not normally this shy."

I planted a smile on my face and whispered to Travis, "I thought it was just a call. I didn't know she could see me." Then I looked at the screen and smiled politely as I could, given my mouth was suddenly very dry. I took a sip of tea. "Hello, Mrs Craig. Sorry to intrude. I didn't realise it was a video chat, and I apologise." I cleared my throat. "I hear it's your birthday. I hope you're having a good day, ma'am."

There was a slight delay and the screen jumped, but the lady on my laptop screen smiled. "Hello, Charlie. It's nice to meet you," she said, her accent mirroring that of her son. "It is my birthday, and seeing Travis is the nicest surprise."

"Well, I hope you have a lovely day," I started, trying to get out of this conversation.

"Tell me," Mrs Craig said. "How's Travis fitting in over there?"

"Just fine, ma'am," I said. "He's fitting in real well."

Travis snorted and whispered, "Like latex." There was no way his mother could have heard it, but I damn near choked on my tea.

Thankfully, I heard Ma in the kitchen starting the breakfast round, so I excused myself and said goodbye. "Pleasure to meet you," I said to Mrs Craig.

I wasn't even to the door when she laughed. "Well, I think it makes sense now," she said. "Why it had to be that ranch—"

"It's called a station, Momma," Travis corrected her.

It made me smile. Lord knows he'd been corrected on it himself a dozen times. I didn't hear what was said after that;

I went into the kitchen and kissed Ma on the cheek. "Mornin'."

"Hey, love. You're up earlier than usual."

I sipped my tea. "Travis needed to use my laptop. It's his mother's birthday." I realised I'd just kind of given myself away. "He, uh, he woke me up. Didn't want to just use it without asking."

"Hm mm," Ma hummed in that *of-course-he-did-I-ain't-stupid* tone she always used when she knew damn well I was lying. "Can you get the bacon out of the fridge for me?"

I loved how she never pushed. I put my tea down and helped her—or more or less got in her road—until Travis was standing in the door.

I leaned against the table. "Everything good back home?" I asked.

His smile became a grin. "Yep."

"Do you miss them?" I asked. "Feeling homesick?"

"My mom's making everyone visit her great-aunt today. Said it's *her* birthday, they'll all do what *she* wants," Travis said. "Which is fine, but my great-aunt smells like pureed food and mothballs and insists on serving a cold fish dish that no one really knows what's in it." He frowned and shuddered like he could still taste that memory. "So no, being at home is the last place on the planet I'd want to be right now."

Ma laughed. "And here I was going to serve cold fish for breakfast."

"That's fine," Travis said, looking over the pan on the stove. "As long as it looks and tastes like bacon."

I put my cup of tea to my lips to hide my smile, he looked right back at me and for a good long while, we just stared.

"There's more coffee here," Ma told him, seemingly oblivious to the way we were looking at each other.

Travis refilled his cup, then looked at me and mouthed the words, "My mom thinks you're cute."

I narrowed my eyes and gave a sharp, pointed nod toward Ma, silently telling him to behave.

He grinned and mouthed the words, "So do I."

I took a calming breath, but I could feel my cheeks heating up. He thinks I'm cute. *Fucking hell.* I mouthed, "Shut up."

He glanced around the room. "It's the kitchen," he mouthed. "I can say what I want."

I growled at him and his laugh made Ma turn around. She looked from me to him, knowing damn well something was going on between us, and tried not to smile. "Boys, set the table for me."

We did as she asked, and when George and everyone else came in for breakfast, Travis was back to basically ignoring me. Which was exactly what I'd asked him to do, so it was fine. But then halfway through eating, a foot hooked around the back of mine. He kept on eating and never missed a beat, but there in front of everyone, though no one could see, he went and did that. It was kinda like holdin' hands, except with feet.

No one else would have known any different. He was acting so normal, I would have wondered if it was even *his* foot but for the fact he was sitting right next to me. That and the real slight way the corner of his mouth curled upwards in an *I-know-a-secret* kind of smile.

Something about his foot-holding gesture, something about him, made my heart thump funny. I pretended to sip my tea, but really I was just hiding my smile and catching my breath.

After breakfast when everyone else was gone and we were heading out the door, I grabbed my hat off my hook and got stuck staring at the empty hook on the right—where my father's hat used to hang.

Travis stood beside me, holding the hat I'd leant him. "It's not just an empty hook, is it?" he asked quietly.

I looked at him, then to the floor. I couldn't answer.

"Dunno what scares me more," he murmured. "The fact that hook just sits there empty, or the way you look at it."

I took a reflexive step away from him—away from his words—shoved my hat on my head, pushed the screen door open and walked outside.

I was busy all day anyway, fixing fences in the holding pens, so it wasn't like I was deliberately avoiding him. But when he was around with the other guys, I pretended to be really busy.

His words had stung.

Not because of the truth that was in them, but because they came from him.

Things weren't supposed to be getting personal between us. Which was ridiculous, because every night for the past week, things got awfully personal between us.

I was having a hard time differentiating the two. Travis on the other hand, seemed to take it all in stride. I was all out of sorts, which I put down to bein' all out of practice. I wasn't used to physical stuff: the touching with hands and feet and the kissing and nose nudges. It gave me butterflies for the pure and simple reason that I wasn't used to it.

It had been years since I'd been part of any of that.

Travis was all handsy and touchy-feely because he was used to it. He must have done it all the time with other guys. I mean, he was in Sydney for four days, slept for one of 'em and used two condoms in the two days before coming out here. Apparently he was very used to bein' all friendly with other guys.

Which was something I tried real hard not to think about, because it made me cranky.

Like, irrationally pissed off. Which was stupid. As if the blistering sun and two thousand head of cattle weren't enough to worry about, I spent the day trying to push down all these feelings and shit that I wasn't rightfully prepared to deal with.

Then at dinner time, Travis wouldn't look at me again. Not in a deliberate *so-they-don't-suspect-anything* kind of way, but in a *I-shouldn't-have-said-what-I-said* kind of way.

I kept up the *ignoring-him-because-he's-doing-my-head-in* gig I had down pat until the house was quiet and I thought he'd gone to bed. I sat at my desk, staring at the office wall, when there was a quiet knock on the door. Travis stuck his head in, and probably guessed he could come in when I didn't tell him to leave. He stepped inside and closed the door behind him.

He didn't say anything. He just walked over to where I was sitting, put his hands on either side of my face and kissed me.

It was soft and trembly and when he pulled away, he whispered, "I'm sorry." He still had his eyes closed, and he kissed me again. "I shouldn't have said that this morning. I was out of line and I apologise."

I put my hands up to cover his, taking them from my face but keeping his hands in mine. He looked at me then: his eyes were wide and sorry. "It's okay," I told him.

Still holding his hands, I stood up, but he never took a step back to give me any room. We were standing about as close as we possibly could; I could feel the rise and fall of his chest against mine, our noses were almost touching. And he just kept staring at me.

It was when he did shit like that that made my heart go beatin' itself all out of rhythm.

"Will you please take me to bed?" he whispered.

I'd barely nodded when he pulled my hand and led me to the door. He dropped my hand when he walked out into the foyer, I presumed in case anyone was out there. But as soon as I followed him into my room, he turned and shut the door, pushing me up against it.

He was all over me. His hands, his mouth. It was heady to be so wanted, even if it was only a physical desire, it still felt fucking great.

I pushed us off the door and stepped him toward the bed, but then with my hands to his face, I pulled his lips from mine, struggling to catch my breath. "Travis, we need to stop."

I could barely make his features out in the darkened room, but I could see the confusion and hurt as clear as day. He took a step back.

"Um," I said, still a little breathless. "We can't have sex tonight. You've got five days in saddle," I told him. "Your arse will be sore enough. You can be pissed at me all you like now, but at the end of the week, you'll be thanking me."

He pouted and huffed. He knew I was right, he just didn't like it.

I walked around him and kissed the back of his neck. I lifted the hem of his shirt and pulled it over his head, throwing the t-shirt to the floor so I could kiss down the bare skin of his shoulder. "I never said you couldn't come."

His head fell back and I kissed his neck, savouring the heat, his smell, the way his breath hitched when I scraped my teeth on his skin. Five days mustering, five days with everyone around, night and day, five days with no chance of escape, five days without feeling him in my arms or the soft touch of his lips.

"Five days," he said. I wondered if I'd said it out loud or if he'd read my mind.

Or if he was just thinking the same thing as me.

"Five days," I repeated. I moved around his side, kissing his arm, then to his front, kissing his chest, his collarbone and his neck.

"That's a really long time," he said breathily. "Without... this."

"It is," I said, spreading my fingers wide on his sides, slowly raking over his skin, trying to relish every touch, every second, everything.

I ran my nose up his neck and over his jaw before I kissed him. I pushed him onto the bed and kissed down his chest and took him into my mouth. I brought him to the brink quickly, and his whole body shook when he came. Still convulsing and writhing, he pulled me by the tops of my arms so I could hold him.

He snuggled into me, which I was learning was a Travis thing to do, one of his touchy-feely things he did so well, and we lay like that for a long time. I refused to overthink things between us. All it did was mess with my head. I must have just dozed off at some point, but even in my sleep-riddled haze, I felt a warm, wet sensation engulf my dick.

I jerked awake and he was quick to put his hands on my chest. When I looked down, Travis had his mouth open over my half-hard cock and he smiled before sliding back down.

I fell back against my bed and let him have his way with me. I didn't try and draw it out or prolong the pleasure; I just let it consume me. I let him consume me. It wasn't long before I came, making Travis hum around me.

He crawled up my sated body and nestled his face into my neck, and my arms automatically went around him. "That was disappointing," he said.

I opened my eyes. "Huh?"

"It went straight down my throat," he said seriously. "I didn't get to taste it."

Boneless and sleepy, I still burst out laughing. "Terrible shame."

"It is," he said. "I might have to wake you up in the morning and try it again."

I fell asleep with a smile, and true to his word, that's exactly what he did.

CHAPTER EIGHT

HORSES SHOULD DO A LOT OF THINGS. COMING HOME ALONE AIN'T EVER ONE OF THEM.

I'D ALWAYS LOVED DROVING cattle, especially as a kid when my dad would let me ride along with George.

And for all the solitude and loneliness this place brought with it, this was what I loved.

This is what I was born to do.

And there was something comforting in knowing—without any doubt—what you were put on this earth for.

The seven of us headed out after breakfast, me in the chopper, four on horseback, three on bikes, with two extra horses laden with swags, food, fuel and water. Shelby was saddled and tethered along for if and when I needed her. The thing about droving cattle in the Outback is that it hadn't really changed a great deal in a hundred years. Well, apart from the introduction of dirt bikes, helicopters and GPS, it still took several men and women, and it still took a week. We still spent long days in the baking sun and cool nights, still sat around campfires under an entire sky of stars.

Out there in the absolute definition of open space was also the closest I felt to the people who worked for me, who helped me make Sutton Station what it was. There was a level of trust we put in each other out here, and mustering was the pinnacle of that.

On the first day, we'd started at the most northern boundary and started to come down, gathering the mob of cattle as we pushed south. It was the same route I'd been on twice a year, every year. It was the same route my father used. We'd come down the dry Arthur River bed into the also dry Lucy Creek and bring them home from there.

The landscape, baked under a scorching sun for a million years, was unchanged but ever different. From my seat in the chopper, I envied those on horseback. Even as hot as it was, there was something about sitting in a saddle, setting off for days in this godforsaken land that soothed me.

I took the chopper west and did a sweep for any cattle that hadn't come across. Closing the water off up the tops a few weeks earlier did most of the hard work for us, since they started to come down on their own, but there was always a few that strayed. But it meant the distance they still had to travel was a good fifty kilometres. It was slow going on the ground on bikes and horses, but they handled it beautifully.

It was like Travis had done this his whole life, and even from my seat in the chopper I could see the smile on his face as Texas would break into a canter to round up a steer or two that'd broken out of the mob.

I kept an eye on him that first day, making sure he knew what he was doing and didn't go off doin' anything reckless. But he kept his cool, laughing most of the day, and did it all like he was born out here. He never hesitated, always the first to give Texas a nudge and shoot off to keep a few wayward cattle in line.

To be honest, I didn't know if the way he adapted to the

Outback so completely was a surprise, or knowing him, if it didn't surprise me at all.

Bringing two thousand head of cattle down a dry river bed in forty-degree heat should have sent most men packing. But not him. He thrived.

I went back to the homestead the first night. I needed to refuel the chopper, but I landed in a clearing close by and made sure everyone was right, that bikes had fuel and horses had feed and water, that the cattle were settled and the campfire was lit and food was cooking.

Even with the comforts of home instead of a swag on the hard ground, I wished I was there with them and not in my soft bed. It wasn't that as the owner and financial bearer of the cattle I lacked trust in my staff—it wasn't that at all. I just loved being out there.

And Travis was there. And I... wasn't.

So the next day, before the sun was up, I took George in the chopper with me, instead of him driving the Land Rover out. Ma loaded up fresh supplies and drove it herself. That way George could take over the chopper and leave me on the ground with my crew.

Shelby was one of the spare horses, already saddled because it was always the plan that I'd be joining them. It was just a day earlier than intended.

And as soon as we had the camp packed up, I was in the saddle and we were pushing the mob south. We'd arranged a rendezvous point with Ma for supplies and lunch and kept on with the slow drove south.

THAT NIGHT AROUND THE CAMPFIRE, we'd laid out our swags when we were getting ready for sleep. We were all kind of spread out around the fire, but Travis had put his closest to mine. He was still about six feet away from me and as we finally lay down for some shut-eye, he rolled over and faced me. To anyone else, he would have looked sound asleep, but he just lay there with his eyes open, looking at me. He'd smile every now and then and his blinks got longer, but he still just stared at me.

I guess I looked right back at him. If I couldn't feel him next to me, asleep in my bed, then this was the next best thing. He didn't have his arms around me, he wasn't sprawled out, hogging my bed, there were no sleepy kisses to my chest. But the way he just lay there looking at me kinda made me feel like he was.

We didn't say anything—we were supposed to be asleep—but we just lay there looking at each other. Everything was quiet, except for the cattle and the sound of someone snoring—and the hammering of my heart.

I don't know which one of us fell asleep first.

THE NEXT DAY was the same, as was the night that followed. During the day, he had Texas turning on command like he'd hand-raised him, and at night we fell asleep just staring at the other.

On the third day, I woke up as hard as the ground I slept on. Watching Travis in the saddle, rising up, pushing with his thighs and the way the muscles in his forearms flexed under his rolled-up sleeves almost had me stir-crazy and aching, aching for relief.

As we bought the cattle down closer to home, to what would be our final temporary holding yard before we penned them, George had been scouting back to give any stragglers a push forward. "There's still a few steers lagging," he said over the radio. "But I gotta go refuel."

"No worries," I told him. "You go home. We'll get 'em." I pulled Shelby around and, while I grabbed some supplies, two swags and some water, told the others I'd have to head back to the rear of the herd and keep them gathered. Before anyone else could offer, I said, "Travis. You're with me."

I LOADED SHELBY, settled back in the saddle and took off north, knowing he'd be right behind me. It wasn't long until I could hear a horse following. I knew Travis was smiling without having to turn around. Between us, we easily rounded the last of the stray steers up before dusk and brought them back to the herd, but instead of heading back to camp, I headed the other direction.

Travis never questioned me, just rode alongside me.

"Don't you want to know where we're going?" I asked.

He grinned at me. "Nope. Just happy for some—" He shifted in his saddle. "—alone time."

I laughed. "Is that what they're calling it these days?"

"I believe so," he said. "I'm pretty sure I read in the travel brochures that you could come out to the Outback for some alone time. But I'm not sure it included some hot station owner whose ass in those jeans in that saddle have been driving me insane for three days."

Now it was me who shifted in my saddle, and I couldn't stand it a minute longer. I pulled on the reins, bringing Shelby to a stop, swung my leg over and slid off her. I looked up at Travis, who was still smiling, still sitting up on Texas. "Can you get down?"

He chuckled as his grin widened. "What for?"

"Because if I climb up there, we might cross some animal husbandry line that rightfully shouldn't be crossed."

Travis burst out laughing, but he threw his leg over and slid down so he was standing in front of me, in between the two horses. He was still smiling, but now his eyes were darker. He looked... hungry.

My mouth was dry, it was fucking hot, we were covered in a fine red dust and we must have smelled like something terrible, but I didn't care.

I stepped toward him and put my hands on his neck, just about to pull him in for a kiss when he stopped me.

He looked back the way we'd come. "How far away from camp are we?"

"Far enough," I said. My voice was rough and my patience was low. I leaned in again, needing to kiss him, but he pulled back. I almost snarled at him. "I've wanted you for three days."

He smiled, all casual and smug. "Just three?"

I couldn't stand the ache, the need any longer. I dropped my hands from his neck and palmed my dick.

This time Travis grabbed my face and pushed me a step backward, up against Shelby. He smashed his mouth to mine. It was a hard kiss; our teeth clinked and our tongues collided. He gripped my face so tight it almost hurt. I could taste his desperation—or maybe it was mine.

His hands were all over me, his fingers digging into me as he pushed against me. He gripped my ass and pulled our hips together, making both our tongues still and stutter. Then he was fumbling with my belt buckle and I let him. I knew what he was after, and I fucking needed it. I'd never needed so bad in my life. Finally, after he undid my jeans, he slid his hand inside.

I groaned as he wrapped his hand around my cock and

pumped me. I bucked my hips, fucking his fist, fucking his mouth with my tongue, and I was so close.

Then he stopped.

His hand was gone, his lips were gone. I opened my eyes to see him go to his knees, looking up at me and smiling.

He pulled my jeans open wider and pulled my cock from my briefs, then slid his tongue over the tip.

"Oh fuck," I whispered. "Suck me."

Travis pressed his lips to the swollen head, then took me in to his mouth, warm and wet, sliding his tongue, sucking me down. I knocked his hat off his head so I could grip his hair and he groaned. The sound snapped any control I had, and I thrust into his mouth and shot my load into his mouth.

My knees gave out. I couldn't stand up, and Travis's hands were on me—I thought to hold me steady. But he let me fall to my knees while my head spun. I gave my dick a squeeze, and my whole body jerked as the last of my orgasm fired through me.

Travis stood up in front of me, and without a word, he undid his belt buckle, then popped the button on his jeans. He pulled the fly open wide and freed his rock-hard cock just a few inches from my face.

Still without speaking, he put his fingers under my chin and lifted my face and fed me his cock.

And I let him. I opened my mouth for him and opened my throat. He held my head, guiding me as he fucked my mouth. He was so hard and swollen, I took every inch he gave me and when I swallowed around him, he thrust one last time and came into my throat.

"Oh fuck, Charlie," he whimpered, unsteady on his feet.

I held his hips as he swayed, grinning up at him. I stood

up and cupped his face as I kissed him, sweeter and softer this time. His eyes were all unfocused and he had that lazy smirk of his.

"Feel better?" I asked him.

"Hm mm," he hummed. "You?"

"Much better."

"I can't believe you led me off away from camp to have your way with me."

Smiling, I stuffed my dick back into my briefs and did up my jeans. "I can't believe I lasted three days."

Travis laughed and looked down at his still-exposed dick. Still hanging heavy and half-hard, it looked like he could almost go again. "We're setting up camp here, yeah? We're not going back to the others?" He glanced at me and grinned. "Should I bother putting this away?" he asked, giving himself a tug.

I groaned and ignored the blatant suggestion. "We'll set camp up here."

He tucked himself back in and chuckled. He took Texas by the reins and led him to a bit of a clearing. "Don't listen to him," he said to his horse. "He didn't mean it about the animal husbandry thing."

"I heard that," I told him, leading Shelby in the same direction.

Travis leaned in to Texas's ear and whisper-shouted so I could hear, "I won't let him try anything. I'll wear him out first, okay, buddy?"

I snorted and he looked back at me and grinned. Then he pretended to speak to Texas again. "No, no. Shelby will be just fine. He won't try anything with her. She's a girl."

This time I laughed. "You're such a dickhead."

He chuckled to himself, stopped walking and started to unsaddle Texas. "Well, the other guys might not be able to see or hear us"—he dumped the saddle and laid out his swag —"but we might teach these cattle a thing or two about sex."

I looked over to the cattle who were finally settling down for the night. "I, um, I don't think Brahman know what a headjob is."

Travis shook his head. "No wonder they have long faces."

I shook my head but couldn't help but laugh. "That's the worst joke ever."

Travis laughed. "But you laughed, so I consider it a win." He took off his hat and threw it on to the saddle, then wiped his brow with his shirt sleeve. "Now before I lay down, is there anything else I need to do? Because I don't think I'll be getting up in any real hurry."

"Are you okay?"

"Okay?" he asked. "I hurt in places I never knew I had. I have saddle rash, and I have red dust in my eyes, up my nose and in my hair. I haven't shaved in three days and my face itches—"

"I like the stubble," I interrupted.

He scratched his face. "Well, too bad. It's not staying."

I laughed. "Are you really sore?"

He stopped and stared at me. "In places I shouldn't hurt... well, not without good reason."

I bit the inside of my lip. "Are you glad now that I said no to sex the night before we rode out?"

"Hell no," he said. "If I was gonna be sore anyway, it may as well have involved sex." He waved his hand at his makeshift bed. "Can I lie down?"

"Be my guest."

Travis almost fell to the ground, slumping onto his swag. "How many times a year do you do this?"

"Twice." I grabbed some nearby dry twigs and brush

and set about starting us a fire. "This is my favourite part of my job." Then I corrected, "Well, of what I do. It's not really a job. It's just my life."

Travis rolled to his side, crooked his arm under his head and watched me. "I can see why you love it."

I smiled as I put some bigger sticks on the fire. "Can you? I mean it must be real different to where you're from."

"It is," he agreed. "But there's something about this place."

His words made me a little nervous; all his talk about the Outback and how much he loved it, seeing him droving cattle with a smile, knowing he fit right in. He was starting to sound like me.

"I'll just put a call in to the others," I said, changing the subject and moving away from the heat of his eyes. I picked up the radio and told Billy where we were. I told him the cattle at the back were restless and we'd camp out here the night and that I'd be in touch in the morning.

"Sure thing, Mr Sutton" was his only reply.

I collected our dinner from the kit of supplies I'd taken from camp, and Travis sighed. "I like Billy."

"He's a good man." I put the pan onto the fire and tipped in the stew to heat. "He's one of the best stockmen I've seen."

"He knows his way out here."

"It's in his blood."

"Like you."

I smiled and stirred the stew. "Yeah, well, I'm pretty sure if you were to cut me, I'd bleed red dirt."

Travis chuckled. "I ain't surprised. That stuff gets into everything." To prove his point, he rubbed his head and a flurry of dust flew out from his hair.

I dished up his portion of meat and dumplings and

handed it to him. He groaned as he sat upright, but thanked me when he took his plate.

"You are seizing up," I said with a laugh.

"I was the first day, but there was no way I was gonna act all hurt in front of the others. I'd never hear the end of it." He took a mouthful of dinner and hummed. "Damn, this is good."

I swallowed my mouthful. "Ma makes a good stew."

"And biscuits."

I looked at my plate. "And what?"

"Biscuits," he repeated, and pushed a damper dumpling with his fork on his plate.

"That ain't no biscuit. That's a dumpling, or a savoury scone, I guess you could call it."

He shook his head. "Man, you have weird names for things out here."

I laughed. "Do me a favour. When you see Ma, tell her you liked her biscuits. But just make sure I'm there to see it."

Travis smiled as he chewed. "No thanks. Lesson number one: don't piss off the cook."

"Actually, lesson number one is don't piss off the boss."

He looked at me and chuckled. "Nah, I think I got him all figured out."

I swallowed my mouthful and, avoiding his gaze, looked back to my plate. "Is that right?"

He just hummed and kept eating his dinner. I hated the way he made me so damn nervous, the way his eyes could see right into me, and the way he could just say something that would throw me so off guard. I threw my paper plate into the fire. "I'll just see to the horses," I said quietly, leaving him to finish eating.

I gave Shelby and Texas some water and some chaff,

and Shelby gave me a nudge goodnight. When I walked back over to the fire, my bed was a lot closer to Travis's than it was when I left it.

He shrugged unapologetically. "You were too far away."

Getting ready for bed, I pulled off my boots. "You're gonna want to get under your netting or the mozzies will eat you alive."

"Mozzies?"

"Mosquitoes," I answered.

"Weird names," Travis mumbled, shaking his head. He pulled off his boots then his shirt, but instead of getting into his own bed, he jumped over and got into mine. He held back the top cover with the netting, said nothing but smiled.

"Travis," I started. "We shouldn't. What if one of the others comes looking for us early?"

"I never said I was spending the whole night in your bed," he said flatly. "Though it's nice of you to ask, I don't think we should in case one of the others comes looking for us early."

I laughed and sighed, and figuring it would be easier not to argue, I got into bed. Well, I tried to. "These swags really aren't made for two."

Travis wriggled until we were squashed in and he was on top of me. "We *do* fit."

I laughed. "You're impossible."

We had to shuffle a bit and I spread my legs as wide as the swag would allow so he fit snug in between my thighs. He deliberately ground his hips into me, pushing his hard-on against mine. His lips were at my neck. Jesus, he would be the death of me.

"Charlie," he whispered.

"Yeah?"

"You taste like red dust."

I laughed and he latched his mouth onto my shoulder. I rolled my hips into his and ran my hands over his ass. Our cocks pressed between us, rutting and sliding, and I slid a hand between us and took both shafts in one hand.

Travis tried to give me as much room as he could, and he kissed over my chest, sucking and nipping the skin while we fucked my fist. Only when we were both close to coming did he kiss me. Slow, sweet and sleepy kisses.

When we were done and cleaned up, Travis reluctantly got back into his own swag. "Oh my god," he whispered.

"What?"

"Look at the sky."

The Outback night sky was truly something special. Whether it was the dark of the desert or the vast flatness of it, I didn't know. But I swear you could see every star. "It's beautiful, isn't it?"

"I have never seen anything like it."

I chuckled at him. "You've been sleeping under that sky for days. How have you not noticed it?"

"I've been too busy looking at something else," he said. "I'd call it beautiful, but he'd get a fat head."

I snorted, grateful he couldn't see me blush. "I've been called a lot of things. That ain't ever been one of 'em."

He turned to look at me for a long moment, like he was gonna say something but didn't. He looked back to the countless stars instead. Then he told me stories of when he was a kid growing up in Texas and sleeping in the backyard, how he'd dreamed of camping out like this.

He talked until he was falling asleep, and I just lay there and looked at him. Even when he'd finally stopped talking, I watched him sleep against the flickering light of the fire.

I'd jumped into raging rivers, ridden wild bulls, bucking horses and fought off deadly snakes. I'd done a thousand crazy things in my life that made Ma yell at me, but I'd never—*never*—been as scared as I was when I looked at him.

THE NEXT MORNING, we kept pushing south toward our final destination. We joined back up with the crew and I went to the head of the mob and led them toward home. There was an excitement amongst my staff knowing we were almost done and that we'd done the job well.

By midafternoon, when George rode up to meet me, I knew we were close. I radioed back to Billy, my lead stockman, and told Fish and Bacon to close in from the rear. This was the tricky part of the muster, this is where it could all go wrong. I had no doubt George had the gates all open and the water and molasses blocks out. All going well, we'd lead them in through the first open gates in a funnel-formation and draft them into sectioned yards when we had them all penned in.

The fenced area was huge—about four acres in itself— and there were four different fenced sections, each with water troughs and molasses and one-tonne bales of hay.

We'd done this plenty of times and had it down to an art, and when we'd finally had the mob all in, the gates were shut and the cheers went up. Not even the baking heat was dampening the mood. But now was when the real work began.

"Trudy, Fish and Travis, check the fences and how the cattle are coping." I called out. "Bacon, Billy, start weeding the bulls out into the first yard. Water your horses first. It's hot and I don't want undue distress. George and I will start on separatin' the steers."

Getting the herd settled before nightfall was paramount. George took the chopper up doing a final scout for strays, and Billy, Ernie and Fish were making sure the calves and yearlings weren't distressed. Mick and Bacon were doing slow laps around the holding yard in the Land Rover and on bikes, Travis and Trudy had taken the horses to be unsaddled, watered, fed and rested.

Always the last in, I'd just gotten off Shelby, feeling every ache in my body and very relieved that we were home without injury. Travis took Shelby's reins and Ma came out to see us.

"You boys look exhausted," Ma said. "I promise dinner'll be something special, then you can sleep."

I smiled at her, just as George's voice cracked over the radio. "Got six or seven steers headed northeast, about three miles from home."

Shit.

Six or seven. I considered letting them go, but then Travis was beside me, still holding Shelby's reins. "I'll get 'em."

I ignored his offer and pressed the radio intercom. "Billy? Where you at?"

He took a while to answer. "Got a problem with the second bore, boss. I'll have it fixed real soon."

"I can get them," Travis said again.

This time I looked at him and sighed. "Alright. Take Shelby."

Travis grinned from ear to ear, climbed up into the saddle and led her out of the yard.

When I looked back at Ma, she was trying not to smile. "You let him ride Shelby?"

I couldn't help but smile. "Don't start." I pressed the radio again. "George? We got bore problems. Can you head in?"

His reply was immediate. "On my way."

I spent the next few hours fixing the bore with George, my arms in mud and grease, in a holding yard with two thousand cattle. The heat, the smell was stifling. But without water, these cattle would die and it was a risk I wasn't prepared to take.

When George and I walked back to the house, it was getting on dark and dinner time. Everyone was out the front in the shade talking quietly, and I knew something was wrong.

Travis wasn't there. No one had seen him. He hadn't come home.

"Gear up," I ordered them. All of them. "We'll need to go out and look for him. He was headed northeast just three miles out. He can't be too far. Take radios, take water, we'll fan out and—"

"Boss!" Billy called out. "Boss! Look!"

I stood beside him, looking out to the direction he was calling. Then I saw what he saw. A riderless horse came trotting into the yard. She stomped her foot and shook her head.

Shelby.

And no Travis.

CHAPTER NINE

LOST AND FOUND, AND THE CRUMBLING OF WALLS.

A COLD DREAD filled my belly, and I could barely speak. Travis was out there somewhere, God only knew where. He could be, and more than likely would be, injured.

If he wasn't already dead.

I didn't want to let my staff see how worried I was, how there was a very real fucking panic bubbling just under the surface. I wanted to scream and punch something, and if I could kick my own ass for letting him go alone, I would.

"I'll take the chopper," I told them. "George, you're on the spotlight."

He gave a nod and disappeared out the door.

It was getting darker and I knew this would be hard going, but we had to do something. We couldn't just leave him out there.

I told everyone to saddle up, horses only, no bikes. Given it was dark, we needed to listen more than look, and if Travis called out, the sound of his voice would be drowned out by the bikes. Everyone did as I asked, no one complained, even though it was probably the last thing they felt like doing. They hadn't rested, they hadn't eaten, but I didn't care. They knew if it were any of them in Travis's place right now, they'd want us to come looking for them too.

"Stay on the radio," I told them. I looked at my watch. It was going on eight o'clock. "We go for two hours and then meet back here. You stay on open radio lines the whole time. I don't want to be looking for one of you as well."

Ma looked as worried as I felt. She was staying at the homestead in case for some miraculous reason, Travis walked in by himself. "What about the cattle?" she asked, giving a pointed glance to the holding yard. "What if they get out?"

My answer was simple. "Let them go."

My team knew what I was saying. I'd forfeit six months income to get the lost man home again. I couldn't look any of them in the eye. I didn't want them to see how close I was to losing it. They rode out, and when I got to the chopper, George was in the pilot seat. "I'm flying. You're on the light."

"I'm all right to fly," I said with more bite in my tone than I should have.

George put his hand over mine to stop them from shaking. "Charlie," he said calmly. "We'll find him."

I didn't say anything—I certainly didn't argue. I just climbed into the passenger seat and waited for him to take us up. Once up in the air, I scanned the spotlight over the darkened ground, looking at the shrubs, the thickets looking for him.

We searched up ahead of those on horseback, up to about ten kilometres from home. We did a kind of grid, sweeping back and forth, searching with the spotlight, hoping to catch a glimpse of something that shouldn't be there.

Travis.

With every pass, with every turn of the grid, panic and fear tightened in my chest and a sinking feeling of hopelessness took hold in my heart. Every time the radio crackled, hope would spike in my blood, only to be crushed when someone said they found nothing.

"We'll need to head back," George said. "We're at ten percent."

"One more pass," I said.

"It's been one more pass four times."

"One more!"

George didn't argue again, he turned the chopper around and we headed a little farther out.

We found nothing.

"I have to take her in," George said. "We'll be lucky to get home as it is."

I nodded, knowing he was right. I just kept scanning the ground, hoping we'd missed him, hoping we'd find him.

We didn't.

When we got back to the homestead, everyone was already there. They'd eaten without us, and I was grateful for Ma for insisting they did. I needed to be the boss, I needed to keep my shit together and act like I was in complete control.

I avoided Ma's eyes, knowing if I saw her worry, her sadness, my flimsy hold on control would fall apart. "We'll head out again first thing," I told them. "Be here at five." I was going to leave it at that, but needed to reassure them. "You all did real good this week. You're the best there is, and I'm grateful. But you need to sleep," I told them. "And tomorrow we'll find him."

They were quiet, and they all gave me a nod on their

way out, but Billy stopped. "I'll take care of Miss Shelby, boss?"

"Leave her saddled," I said quietly. I said they had to sleep. Not me.

"Charlie," George said with half a warning in his voice. "You can't go out at night. It's too dangerous."

I turned to face him, and whatever he saw in my eyes made him do a double take. There would be no argument.

I walked past George and Ma into my office and rifled through the filing cabinet. I found the old and yellowed papers and took them out to the dining table. I unfolded the maps and without a word, George was beside me.

"He has to be here," I said, pointing to the map. "Inside the first northern paddock. If he was gone for three hours, he can't have gone farther than that. Not on Shelby. Even if she ran full gallop for three hours"—I drew a circle around the target search area—"he has to be in here."

George nodded again. "It's not too cold tonight, but tomorrow will be another hot one. Temps are set to break forty-five tomorrow. I know you want all hands out lookin', but someone should stay here to keep an eye on the cattle. I'd say Billy, but out of anyone here, you want him on that search party. Bacon's capable of mindin' the mob. The rest of us can look for Travis."

Forty-five degrees in the desert sun. No water. No shade. Statistically, we had twenty-four hours to find him.

I put my hands on the table and hung my head. "How could I have been so stupid?" I mumbled, not really meaning to say it out loud.

"Travis knows what he's doing," George said matter-of-factly. "He's as good on a horse as any of us. He's taken to bein' here like he was born for it. And he's smart. He'll know what to do."

"I should never have let him go."

"Placin' blame on yourself will do more harm than good, Charlie." George looked at me seriously. "It's not your fault, or anybody's fault, for that matter. Let's not focus on how he got to be out there and let's concentrate on findin' him, huh?"

Ma appeared in the doorway, holding a plate of food. The thought of eating turned my stomach, but I knew I needed to eat—especially if I had no intention of going to sleep. I'd forced down a few mouthfuls when she came back in with a backpack. "Two litres of water, a two-way radio, satellite phone, a flashlight and some more food."

I stood up and put the backpack on. "Thanks, Ma."

"I knew you wouldn't be sleeping," she said. She looked worried. "And let me tell you something else. If you go and get yourself lost or hurt out there, I will search for you myself and kick your arse all the way home, you hear?"

I kissed her cheek, and when I pulled back, her eyes were glassy. "You find him," she whispered.

I swallowed down my emotion and nodded. George walked out with me to where Shelby was tethered. She'd had food and water so I knew she'd be okay even though she was tired. I stood facing her and scratched her ear. "Once more today, girl," I said. She lifted her head and gave me a nudge with her nose. "Did you see a snake? Is that what happened?" I asked her, and she nudged me again. I felt stupid for talking to her, especially in front of George, but Shelby and I always had these kind of conversations. "Can you show me where you left him?"

She didn't answer of course, but George clapped his hand to my shoulder. "You've got four hours. It's going on ten and if you're not home by two, you'll have to answer to Ma."

I gave him a smile, but it was weak at best. I lifted my foot into the stirrup and hauled my tired arse onto Shelby.

We headed out into the darkness, and even though Shelby and I knew these lands better than anyone, I still took it easy. My eyes adjusted to the dark, but the last thing I needed was to get hurt and be a burden on the search for Travis.

I headed northeast, the same direction Travis headed, the same direction Billy and the others headed out looking for him. He had to be out there somewhere. The only problem was, there was an awful lot of somewhere out here.

When I was about a kilometre from the house, I waved the flashlight, hoping he'd see it, and then I started to call his name. I knew over this flat terrain that my voice would carry, and if he was anywhere kind of close, he'd hear me.

I called his name at two kilometres and again at three and four, and probably every few hundred meters in between. By the time I turned east, knowing I had to go home, my throat was raw. And when the only thing that ever called out back to me was dead silence. Knowing I was heading home without him, I couldn't hold back the tears.

All I could think of was how scared he must have been. Wherever he was, he must have been thinking the worst. Not many people survive being lost out here. This land, this fucking red desert, was unforgiving.

He should be sound asleep in bed—in *my* bed—not lying on the ground somewhere scared and alone. I just prayed that he wasn't too badly injured, or worse, bitten by a snake. Given that he'd been missing for well over six hours, if he was bitten by any of the snakes out here, he'd have taken his last breath long before now.

I kicked Shelby in the ribs and urged her home. My thoughts of him all alone out here in the darkness were making it hard to breathe. I needed to cling to whatever hope there was, and I needed to be in charge tomorrow. I needed to regroup, rethink, and set up a search party so we could scour every inch of this fucking place.

By the time Shelby walked into the yard, she was almost dragging her feet. I unsaddled her and led her into the yard where she had feed and water. I took off her bridle and gave her a rubdown on the neck and dragged my sorry self inside.

George met me in the foyer. He didn't have to ask, but I shook my head anyway. His face fell but he nodded and went back to his room.

I stood under the shower for a long while. It had been days since I'd showered and although the water was good on my aching muscles, it did little to improve the ache in my chest. I crawled into my bed and pulled the pillow that smelled of him under my head and stared at the wall until morning.

JUST BEFORE FIVE AM, I picked up the phone and called my neighbour, Greg Pieterson. I knew he'd be up trying to get a day's work done before it got too hot. "Sorry for the early interruption," I said, my voice sounding mechanical, even to me. "But I need your help."

"What is it?"

"We've got a man lost. He's been out there goin' on fourteen hours."

"You sure he's missing?" he asked. Then he corrected himself. "Guess you wouldn't be askin' if you didn't."

"His horse came back without him."

"Oh, shit." There was a muffled sound of voices, like he

put his hand over the receiver. Then he said, "Where do you need me to look?"

We worked out GPS coordinates; if Sutton Station was a clock face, then Travis was somewhere between twelve and four. I'd take the top half, being twelve to two, and Greg could take his chopper and search two to four. We each had about three thousand acres to cover.

We left Bacon to do the job of five people tending the mob of cattle, and we all set out in search of Travis.

I had George with me, and Greg was bringing one of his men with him, because having two sets of eyes up in the air was better than one. The rest of my team were on bikes and horseback in between, and more of Greg's staff were coming across on land.

I flew the chopper at a hundred feet, giving us more visual, considering the size of the land we had to cover. This landscape—red dirt, shrubs and rocks—went for as far as the eye could see. I kept looking through the thickets, hoping to catch a glimpse of his white or blue shirt, hoping he was trying to find shade under the bushes.

This fucking red dirt, the same dirt I swore just the other day that ran through my veins, I'd never hated it so much.

We never saw a thing out of place. Not even the other stray cattle George had spotted. When we'd gone back to refuel before noon, I knew what I had to do.

"Ma, can you do me a favour?" I asked. My throat still hurt.

She looked at me with such sad, sad eyes. "Sure."

"We'll need to put a call in to the Alice police," I said, barely above a whisper. "We need to report him as missing."

She nodded sadly. "Maybe the extra men on the ground will help."

I swallowed hard and whispered, "They won't come as a search and rescue, Ma. They'd just be expecting to retrieve a body."

She shook her head. "They don't know him," she said, lifting her chin. "You just see. He's out there, just waiting 'til we find him."

I gave her a smile I didn't feel. "Sure hope you're right, Ma."

She put both hands on my shoulders. "You will find him."

I couldn't reply to her. There was no way I could get away with false-hoping her. George and I went up again with a whole lot less hope than we did this morning. We followed the grid pattern, liked we'd done before, and came up with nothing. I was getting more and more agitated the longer we were out there, and my heart felt sick.

Then it happened. My radio cracked to life. "Boss," Billy's voice came through. "Boss, I found him."

I snatched up the receiver. "Is he okay? Where are you?" I said, knowing Billy wouldn't have a GPS. "Is he okay? Is he injured? Is he—"

"He's alright," Billy said, cutting in. "Found him at the eastern ridge line, boss."

The eastern ridge line? What the fuck is he doing there? I didn't ask the questions, I just turned the chopper around almost one hundred and eighty degrees and went full throttle. "I'm on my way."

"I'm halfway there," Greg's voice cut in on the radio.

Then Fish's voice. "I'm not far from there."

We were all on the same radio frequency so it was open to everyone. I radioed in for all other crew to head home; he'd been found—injuries unknown—but that I'd bring him back with me. I asked Ma to call the doctor in and to cancel the police, and then I clicked off the handset before Ma shot me any questions. I didn't have the answers anyway, and I wasn't in no state for making conversation. Thankfully George knew when I needed silence, and he gave it.

I didn't know why I let him go on his own. I didn't think about it at all. From the second he arrived, he'd fit in like he'd grown up here. And when those cattle escaped and he jumped at going to bring 'em back, I didn't think for one second he wasn't capable.

I told him to take Shelby—she was still saddled, she was right there.

She was also scared shitless of snakes.

I should have known better. I should have stopped him. I should have said no. I should have done a lot of things different.

The ridgeline came into view first, then I spotted Greg's helicopter. And I could see a group of people around someone lying down, and my chest tightened and my stomach dropped. I brought the chopper around to land, probably too quickly, and we came to ground with a thud. I was out of the chopper before the rotors had stopped turning, and I raced toward them.

All I could see was the man on the ground. They were his boots, it was his shirt. The sight of Travis lying on the ground almost choked me.

Coming to my knees beside him, I forgot all my stupid rules and boundaries and put my hand to his face. "Travis," I said. He looked like shit; his lips were dry, and it was hard to tell if he was sunburned or just covered in red dust. He smiled up at me.

"Don't you fucking smile," I told him. "You scared the shit outta me."

He coughed and closed his eyes. I snatched up the

water canister from beside him and, lifting his head gently, put the water to his lips, giving him only a few drops at a time.

"Saw this," Billy said. When I looked up at him, he was holding Travis's belt buckle. "Was shining on a stick." He must have known the glint of metal could be seen from afar. "Said you told him the ridge was the only shade for miles. Said he knew the shade was here, because the rocks changed colour."

"The limestone ridge," Travis said weakly. "I knew it wasn't far 'cause the sand was tinged with yellow."

I looked back down at Travis. It was all still too much to take in. "We need to get you home."

"My knee's all banged up. Hurts," he said. "More water." I put the canister back to his lips, letting him drink a little more. I could see his knee was swollen, even through his jeans.

I looked up at George, who was now standing near Greg and one of his men we met last week named Johnno. "We'll need two sticks for splints." Then I looked back to Travis. "We'll need to brace that leg before we move you, okay?" He nodded his okay, and it felt like the first time I'd breathed since yesterday. "Wanna tell me what the hell happened?"

"Shelby spooked and threw me," he said, trying to sit up. I helped him and held him steady. I never took my hands off him. "It was a snake. She threw me right at it."

"A snake?"

He sipped more water and nodded. "It was big and brown. From me to you away. Don't know why it didn't strike me."

I exhaled and my chin fell to my chest. I'd never really

been one to believe in a higher power, but I thanked every God ever prayed to right then and there.

"Was it a Taipan? An Inland Taipan or an Eastern Brown?" Billy asked.

"Didn't ask it questions," Travis said. "Just big and brown."

"Either way, Mr Travis," Billy said. "None of 'em are good."

"They're deadly, right?" Travis asked. His blue eyes were tired and his smile was weak. But Jesus, it was good to see him.

Billy laughed behind me and I nodded. "Just a bit, yeah," I said. I don't think he needed to know three brown-coloured snakes out here were some of the deadliest in the world.

George and Greg came back with a few longish sticks; there wasn't much to pick from out here. "These'll have to do," Greg said.

George crouched down to rifle through the medical kit. He must have grabbed it from the helicopter. I didn't even think to bring it...

"Here," he said, holding out some rolled bandage. "This'll have to do."

Travis lay back down, and we put the sticks either side of Travis's leg. As gently as we could, we secured the splints. He hissed in pain as we moved his leg and dug his fingers into my arm harder than I thought was necessary, but he was obviously in a lot of pain. His leg needed to be more secure, so without thinking, I pulled my shirt over my head and wrapped it around his knee, both bracing and securing it.

I lifted Travis's arm around my shoulder and looked up at Billy. "Help me lift him." Billy was quick to comply, mirroring my hold on him. "We're gonna stand you up first," I said to Travis. "Then we'll lift you into my chopper, okay?"

He nodded and grimaced when we lifted him upright. He stood on his good leg, and with his arms around our shoulders, Billy and I each put a hand under Travis's ass and carried him to the chopper.

Using what must have been the last store of energy he had, Travis pulled himself up into the passenger seat. He hissed when he swung his leg in and he paled, a fine sheen of sweat covering his brow, and I knew his leg hurt more than he was letting on.

"You okay?" I asked.

He nodded quickly, not very convincingly. "I for, for—" He breathed out slowly, through the pain. "—forgot my hat."

He was struggling to get his seatbelt buckled, so I took it out of his hands and did it for him. "Don't worry about your hat."

He could barely whisper. "Please."

I shook my head at him, but turned back and stomped over to the others. They were watching me, wondering what was wrong. I picked up his hat and mumbled, "Forgot his fucking hat."

There were a few smiles from them, mostly George. I looked at him. "You alright to get home?"

"I'll double with Fish."

I gave a nod and ran back to the chopper. I climbed in and started her up. Travis had his head back and his eyes were shut. "You okay, Trav?"

"Hmm," he hummed.

"I'll get you home, huh?"

"'Kay."

I took the chopper up and headed home, watching Travis more than the scene in front of me. He kept his eyes closed, his face was sunburned and his lips were dry and chapped. "You scared me," I told him. "You fucking took ten years off me."

With his eyes shut and his head back, I thought he might have fallen asleep, but after a long minute, he said, "I knew you'd find me."

A single tear ran from the corner of his eye, leaving a silver trail over the red dirt on the side of his face. I reached over and squeezed his hand. His fingers latched onto mine and he held on tight until I landed the chopper.

When I landed back at the homestead, we had quite the audience. I got out quickly, before the rotors had fully stopped, and met Bacon at Travis's door. We unbuckled him and lifted him out, carrying him into the house. "My room," I said. Then like I needed to explain why, I added, "It's bigger."

We lay Travis down on my bed and I lifted his leg up and gently put it down on the bed. Ma followed us in with her arms full of medical stuff, water and washcloths. "Doctor's on his way," she said. "Be here in an hour."

She handed me a water bottle and I put it to Travis's lips, giving him small sips at a time. Ma said, "Travis, we need to get these jeans off you, and all tight-fitting clothes. We need to cool you down and get you rehydrated." She left no room for arguments, not that he would have argued with her anyway. He was in no state to do so. "This leg's gonna hurt when we undo this splint," she said. "But we need to do this, okay?"

He nodded at her, but just wanted more water. "Sip it," I told him. "Or you'll be sick."

Ma undid the shirt I'd wrapped around his leg, then the

bandage. I undid his jeans and when we pulled them down and had to lift his leg, he let out a scream through clenched teeth.

He fell back onto the bed, clearly exhausted and spent. His knee was swollen, the skin stretched tight and purple. I don't know if something was broken or just twisted, but it sure looked painful.

"Can we give him something for the pain?" I asked, pulling the sheet up to his waist.

"Not until the doc gets here," Ma said.

Trudy, Bacon and Mick were in the room now, all checking in on him.

"Right, all of you out," Ma said. "I need to get him cleaned up." The others left as quietly as they'd come, then she turned to me and handed me my shirt. "You best put that back on."

I'd been shirtless in front of them a hundred times, I didn't know why now was any different. Ma looked over my chest and I followed her eyes. I had purple marks over my chest and my shoulder. Hickies.

Love bites.

Oh my God.

They'd all seen me. Each and every one of them.

I didn't realise. I didn't even know. It must have been from the night before last when we'd gone away from on our own. We'd spent the night together by the campfire and he'd kissed all over my chest while he lay on top of me. We got up early the next morning, then he'd gone missing. I didn't sleep last night and left this morning before the sun was up. I hadn't looked in a mirror in five days.

Fuck.

They all saw.

There could only be one explanation. The only person

I'd had more than two minutes alone with before Travis went missing was Travis.

They all knew.

Slowly, I pulled the shirt on over my head. Ma was still in front of me. She looked at me with sad eyes. "What you do in your own time ain't none of their business," she said softly.

I suddenly felt every hour since I'd last slept. Tiredness hit me like a ton of bricks. "I'll go get some icepacks for his knee," I said despondently. I walked like an old man into the kitchen and pulled two bags of peas out of the freezer, taking them back to Ma.

She'd wet down a washer and was wiping Travis's face. I put the two bags on the bed beside him, not wanting to go outside to face my crew but knowing I didn't have any choice.

Ma put her hand to my face. "I know you're tired, and you need to shave," she said, scratching my bearded cheek. Then she looked at me seriously, "You're still their boss, so you go out there and be their boss."

Just then the sound of Greg's helicopter interrupted, followed by a motorbike. Everyone, with the exception of Billy—who'd still be riding his horse back—was here. I had no clue what to say, so I took Ma's words about being a boss and walked outside.

Everyone turned to face me just as George and Fish, along with Greg and Johnno, came walking around to the front of the house. "He's kinda sleeping, he's got a busted-up leg and he's real dehydrated. But Ma's with him and the doc will be here soon."

George went inside and no one said anything, so I looked at Greg and Johnno. "Thank you for coming. Thank you."

Greg held out his hand, which I shook. "Anytime."

"Please refuel here," I told him.

He gave a nod. "Lucky kid in there," he said. "Smart. Heading east to the ridge instead of trying to find his way home undoubtedly saved his life."

"I agree," I said. "Not many would have done that. Said he noticed the changes in the colour of different limestone," I said, shaking my head, still nervous that they'd seen the love bites on my chest. Everyone just kind of stood around, and I kept waiting for someone to say something. It was like waiting for the executioner's blade to drop.

But it never came.

Greg and Johnno refuelled their chopper and left, and the others, under my instructions, went back to the holding pen of cattle to check water, food and fences before dinner.

I filled in the hour or so until the doctor got there by avoiding eye contact with everyone and checking the cattle in the holding yards. It was getting hotter and we needed to keep the cattle as cool and as calm as possible. Having so many head of cattle in one confined fenced-off area was not only dangerous to the staff, but also if they weren't treated right, the losses could be devastating.

When the new Land Cruiser pulled up at the house, I made my way over. Tired as hell, I was barely managing one step in front of the other. Doctor Hammond had been the Outback doctor for as long as I could remember. I used to think he was old when I was a kid, and now I wondered whether he aged at all.

There was an esky and his black doctor's bag at his feet. I shook his hand. "Thanks for coming."

"No problem."

"Come inside," I told him. "He's in the first bedroom."

I led Doctor Hammond inside to my room. The door

was ajar but I rapped my knuckles on the old wood door and pushed it open. Travis smiled when I walked in, then looked to the man behind me.

"Travis, this is Doctor Hammond," I said, making quiet introductions. "Doc, this is Travis Craig."

Travis was layin' on his back, dressed only in his undies with the sheet kind of covering his waist but his injured leg was propped up on a pillow, bandaged and with two bags of peas on either side of his knee. He had a wet washer on his forehead and a bottle of water in one hand.

He tried to sit himself up a bit.

"Stay there, son," the doc said. "I hear you've had quite the ordeal."

"Yeah," Travis said. "Something like that."

The doc put the esky and his medical bag on the floor beside the bed.

"You got beer in there?" Travis asked. "'Cause this water just ain't cutting it."

The doc kind of smiled, then took an ear thermometer out of his bag, turned Travis's head and shoved it in ear. "It's an unquenchable thirst, yes?"

"Yeah," Travis said quietly.

He took his blood pressure next, then pupil dilation and then pulled a clear bag of liquid-something out of the esky and some plastic hook-looking thing. He hitched it to the bed head and then set up a cannula in Travis's hand, all the while asking questions about hours and exposure and fluid litreage and how much he'd peed.

"I'll just give you guys a minute," I said quietly, making my way to leave.

"You can stay right there, Mr Sutton," the doc said. "I have questions for you too." The old man turned back to Travis when he inserted the tubes and started the intravenous feed. "Charles never did like needles. Not as a kid, nor as a grown man."

Travis looked over at me and smiled. I rolled my eyes and gave the back of the doctor's head a tight smile, which was probably a sneer, and parked my arse on the dresser.

"Your knee," Doctor Hammond said. "Any movement? Was there a snapping sound or a pop?"

"Don't know," Travis answered. "I was too busy hittin' dirt and countin' the scales on a brown snake to notice."

The doctor smiled this time. In all the years I'd known him, he'd never smiled at me. "I don't need to ask if you were struck by the snake," he mused. "Because you'd be long past needing saline."

"So I've been told," Travis said. Then he said, "It's not broken. I did my ACL playing football a few years back. Feels a lot like that."

The doctor unwrapped the bandage from Travis's knee and inspected the damage. He talked as he did his doctor-thing, asking Travis about America: where he was from and all those type of questions that were a distraction from what he was doing to Travis's knee. When he was done, he said, "Well, I agree. It looks like an anterior cruciate ligament. And you've done a good job of it. No way of knowing without scans, but it's at least a grade-two tear."

While they talked rest and exercise and therapy, I could feel my head getting heavier. I tried to keep my eyes open, but thought I could just rest them for a second while they talked. It wasn't until something in my brain told me I was falling and two hands were on my shoulders, that I jolted awake.

Doctor Hammond's face was peering into mine. "How long since you've slept?"

I blinked a few times and shook my head, trying to clear

some room for thought. "Um, night before last." I shook my head again. "I think."

"Mrs Brown!" the doc yelled. Ma appeared in the doorway. "This man needs food and sleep."

I stood up taller and tried opening my eyes wider. Ma stood beside me and put her hand on my arm. "I'll be alright," I told her.

The doctor ignored me completely. "Mr Craig needs bed rest for a day or two, then he can do some gentle exercise but minimal weight. If the swelling doesn't go down in the next two-three days, take him to hospital."

"Can he fly?" Ma asked.

"Not without wings, Mrs Brown."

Ma smiled, but she looked more worried than anything. "He's supposed to fly back to America in three days."

My gaze shot to Travis and his to me. I'd forgotten all about him leaving... "Three days," someone whispered. I realised a little too late that it was me. I swallowed down the lump in my throat and breathed through the weight on my chest. *How could I have forgotten he was leaving? How could I have not remembered that?*

Ma frowned at me and her eyes were glassy. "Charlie?"

"I forgot he had to go," I told her quietly, almost mouthing the words.

"Charlie," Travis said, but I didn't dare look at him. I just walked out of the room with a hand on the wall to help steady me and walked into the spare room—his room—and lay down on the bed. I closed my eyes, and when I opened them again, it was morning.

My stomach woke me up—I hadn't eaten since god knows when—and it took me a while to get my bearings. I was in a strange bed in a strange room and I was still fully dressed. I was even still wearing my boots. I heard Travis and Ma talking, just the hum of voices, and then I remembered last night.

Travis was flying back to America in three days.

Correction, I thought. *Make that two days.*

I always knew he wasn't here long. In the beginning, we'd even talked about us *having fun* for the few weeks he was here. I'd just not thought of it since.

I guess I kind of got used to him being around.

Knowing I had to face him, I rolled off the bed and walked to my room. I stuck my head in and Ma, who was sitting on the bed next to him, stood up. "I better make a start on breakfast," she said, patting my arm as she quietly slipped out of the room.

I looked at him then, and it felt like my heart was about to stop or burst or something. He'd shaved at some point and looked a lot brighter. His knee was still bandaged and still propped up on pillows, but he was sitting up against the headboard.

"How're you feeling?" I asked him. "You look better."

"I feel better," he said. "You look like shit."

I snorted out a laugh despite my mood. "Thanks."

"You slept in your boots?" he said, nodding toward my feet. "Must have been tired."

I ran my hand through my hair and cleared my throat. "Well, I didn't exactly sleep the night before. Someone got himself lost."

"I wasn't lost," he countered. "I knew where I was. *You* didn't know where I was."

I shook my head. "I thought I was going to have to call your mother," I admitted quietly. "I thought I was going to have to tell her you were—" I took a deep, somewhat shaky breath. "—that you were dead."

Travis patted the bed beside him. I shook my head no.

"Please come sit here," he said.

"I have to get ready," I started to say.

"Charlie, I can't follow you out there so please, please come and sit down."

Something in his tone made me move. I sat on the edge of the bed near his hip and wiped my palms on my thighs.

"Why are you nervous?" he asked. "I thought we were past any reason to be nervous."

I let out a bit of a laugh. "I'm not nervous," I lied.

"Charlie, I was scared as hell out there," he said. "But you know what?"

I looked into his eyes then. "What?"

"I knew you'd find me."

"Well, I wasn't so confident. Hell, I was looking fifteen miles north. I wasn't even close. I don't even know how you got so far out or so far east."

"I was lost," he said, letting his head fall back onto the headboard. "Hopelessly."

"You could have died."

"I know."

"One more day," I told him, shaking my head. "If Billy didn't find you when he did, if you were out there one more night, you'd be dead." I was just about to tell him next time, he was to take water and a satellite phone, but then I realised it didn't matter. There wouldn't be a next time.

He interrupted my thoughts when he reached up and lightly scratched my beard. "Not sure about this. A bit of scruff is good, but a full-on beard is a bit much."

I gave him a smile and went to stand up, but he grabbed my hand. "Thank you," he said softly, sincerely. "Thank you for not giving up. Thank you for looking for me, for stopping at nothing to find me."

"I'd do it for any of my staff," I said, not meaning it how it sounded.

He pulled his hand away and hurt flickered in his eyes. "Right."

I stood up and walked to the end of the bed. "I didn't mean it like that," I said lamely. "I mean, I would look for any of them too, but you were..." I looked out the window as the sun was rising.

"I was what?"

"Different."

"Charlie," he started to say.

I shook my head. "They know, Travis. They know." I ran my hand through my hair again. "They saw me without a shirt. When I wrapped your leg in it. They saw the"—I almost didn't want to say it—"the love bites all over me."

Travis's eyes went wide. "Shit."

Figuring I was about to take a shower anyway, I pulled my shirt over my head. He scanned my chest, seeing the purple blotches he'd left, and his face fell. "I'm sorry."

I shrugged and grabbed some clean clothes from my dresser. "It's done now. I have to face them this morning," I told him quietly. "Knowing that they know." I walked to the door. "Anyway, I guess it doesn't matter."

"What doesn't matter?"

I wasn't going to mention it, but figured it really didn't matter anymore. "You're leaving."

"Charlie."

"I've got a busy day," I said, louder this time. "I need to separate this mob of cattle. I've got three road trains turning up tomorrow, and I can't afford to not be ready."

I turned and left him at that, had a shower and a shave and with a sense of dread, walked out for breakfast. Everyone at the table was kind of quiet, apparently not real sure what to say, myself included. Apparently Ma had told them that Travis was okay but wouldn't be any help in the yard.

There were a few looks around the table, but no one else mentioned him or the marks they'd seen on my chest and shoulders yesterday. I was grateful. After a full breakfast, I gave orders and directions for the day. We needed to draft the herd into their separate yards: steers, heifers, weaners, killings and keepers.

We'd all done it before. We all had roles and responsibilities, and when breakfast was done, everyone went straight to work. The house was quiet, and I breathed a sigh of relief that nothing had been said about me and Travis.

Ma met me in the hall. "Charlie, hun, you okay?" she asked.

"Sure, Ma," I said. "I'm fine."

I was expecting her to call me out on lying, but she didn't. "Okay," she said softly. "If you need to talk, you know where to find me."

I gave her a smile. A very genuine smile. "Sure thing." I turned and walked to front door, but something stopped me.

Travis's hat.

It was on the hallstand, sitting from when it was thrown there yesterday. Like it could have bitten me, I slowly picked it up and brushed it off, and sat it back down on the hallstand, all neat like.

I looked back at Ma, who'd been watching me the whole time. I snatched my hat off the hook, put it on and walked out the door.

WE WORKED all day in the holding yards, separating cattle, penning and tagging. It was stinking hot, over forty degrees, we were sweaty, the horses were sweaty, and by dinner time we were beat.

Too busy all day for conversation and then too hungry to talk at dinner, I'd almost forgotten that they'd all seen the marks Travis had left on me. No one brought it up, so they either didn't care or didn't realise what they were or who put them on me. Either way, I was grateful.

When I'd slumped into my office chair at the end of the day, Ma called out to me. "Charlie? Can you come here?"

I got up and found her in my room, helping Travis out of bed. Ma had a crutch in her hand. "What are you doing?" I asked.

"I'm going stir-crazy in this room," he said, sitting on the edge of the bed. Both feet were down, but he favoured his bandaged leg. "And I need to pee."

"He doesn't want me to take him," Ma said.

"I've had to pee in a bottle all day. Let me have some dignity," he said, looking up to her with a smile.

"I found your old crutch in the shed, from when you broke your leg," Ma said. "But only one of them. Don't know what happened to the other one."

"I tried using it as a diving board when the creek was in flood when I was fourteen, remember?" I told her.

"Hmm," she hummed. "Yeah, and they had to fish you out half a mile down. I remember that part alright."

Travis chuckled, but then he tried to stand up. Ma grabbed him, but I grabbed him too. "You'll be dizzy a while," I told him. "Let your head get used to bein' upright."

He fisted the shirt at my shoulder, and Ma stuck the crutch under his right arm. He took a few deep breaths and said, "I'm right."

I didn't let go of him though. I kept my hand around his back as we shuffled down the hall, and by the time we got to the bathroom, Ma was gone. After he'd peed enough to make the Todd River flow, he leant against the basin. He washed his hands, his face, then brushed his teeth.

I stood and watched him. "Feel better?"

"So much better," he said. He shuffled around on his good foot and reached over and leaned into me. "Didn't just think I was using the excuse to take a piss to get you alone, did you?"

"Not after seeing how long you peed for, no."

He laughed quietly, and then he looked right into my eyes and whispered, "I've wanted to feel your arms around me for two days."

And I couldn't have not done it even if I tried. *Just one last time*, I told myself. Just one last time. This was it, forever. The rest of my life, alone in the middle of nowhere, with only memories to comfort me.

I slowly slid my arms around his waist, careful not to bump his leg. I needed to commit this to memory: the feel of him against me, his arms around me, his hands touching me, his smell.

And when he pulled back a little so he could kiss me, I let him.

Savour it, Charlie, I told myself. *Because this is it.*

Every detail, the softness of his lips, the stubble on his chin, the taste of tongue.

I put my hand to his face and cupped his jaw, slowly ending the kiss. I kept my forehead against his and my eyes closed, savouring the hammering of my heart and not wanting it to end. When I finally opened my eyes, he was smiling.

"Can I watch TV?" he asked.

The question threw me completely. There I was, having a moment I would remember forever, and he was thinking of some crap on television.

"Um, sure," I said. I grabbed the crutch for him and put it under his right arm. I helped him out the lounge room, lowered him into a chair and handed him the remote. "Can I get you a drink or something?"

He shook his head. "Wanna watch something with me?"

"No," I said quietly. "Gonna turn in. It's been a big day. I'm beat."

"Okay," he said. "Sorry. It's just that I've been sleeping most of the day. And I'm wide awake now."

"Well, let me know if you need anything." I turned to walk out.

"Charlie, did anyone say anything to you today?" he asked, stopping me before I could leave. "You know, about the"—he waved his hands across his chest—"love bites?"

I shook my head. "No."

He smiled. "Well, good. I guess."

I turned to the foyer. "I'll take the spare room again," I said quietly. "Give a yell if you need me. If not, I'll see you in the morning."

I showered, and when I crawled into bed, I could hear the TV. Sleep didn't come easily. I lay there, half hoping, half dreading that he'd show up in the doorway. But he never did.

I don't know what bothered me the most: the fact he didn't seem to care that he was leaving or the fact that I did.

THE NEXT MORNING, I didn't see Travis. I presumed he slept late or Ma served him breakfast in bed. Either way, considering what we had going on in the yard, I was glad he wasn't distracting me.

The three road trains—a B-Double truck, each pulling three double-decker trailers—came in midmorning. We had to load each truck with separate yards of cattle, and with over eight hundred head of cattle to haul, it was a huge job.

It was hot, dusty and hectic.

I didn't even notice Travis standing on the veranda. I had no clue how long he'd been there for, but I guess with the noise and the excitement, he didn't want to miss it. It was quite a sight to see, I guess.

He watched us well into the afternoon, standing there leaning on the crutch. I watched him as he stared at the stairs off the veranda, and like I could read his mind, I knew what he gonna do. He balked at the top step, tried putting the crutch on the first step, but then backed up. In the end, after deciding the stairs were too hard to navigate, he kept his leg out in front of him, lowered his ass to the decking boards and swung his legs over the edge. He simply picked up the crutch and started to walk up to the yard.

George was watching me watch him. I shook my head. "Bloody stubborn," I mumbled.

George turned back to the holding yard, but I could see the smile from the corner of his face.

Travis just stood at the fence, leaning against the railing, like he couldn't help himself, like he just had to be a part of it.

And at the end of the day, he simply walked back to the veranda, threw the crutch up first, lifted himself up onto the decking and swung his legs up.

It was one thing that both amazed me and drove me

crazy: once he'd made his mind up, there was no telling him otherwise.

That night, when everyone else had gone to bed, we were in the lounge room and Travis told me he'd spoken to his parents. He'd told them all about his overnight adventure lost in the Outback, about his injured knee, and how we'd rounded the cattle into the corrals and loaded them onto big-ass trucks.

"We don't call them corrals," I reminded him.

"Corrals, holding yards, whatever," he said, rolling his eyes.

"Bet they were glad you're heading home," I said, keeping my tone light.

"Can we talk about that?" he asked. "About me leaving?"

"Not sure what there is to say," I said quietly. My chest was tight and my mouth was dry. "I mean, we always knew you weren't gonna be here for long. I just forgot, I guess..."

"You looked a bit shocked the other night when Ma said I was leaving in three days."

"Well, now it's one day," I said.

Travis grinned at me. He fucking grinned. I felt sick, and he was all happy smiles.

I stood up. "Jesus, Travis. Maybe you could act like you give a shit. I mean, you're leaving here tomorrow and you don't even care." I ran my hand through my hair like I always did when I was stuck for words. "I dunno, you said it was just some holiday fun. I don't know what I was think-ing..." I walked to the door.

"Charlie," he called out, and I stopped.

"I don't care that I'm supposed be leaving tomorrow," he said. "Because I'm not."

I stared at him, turning his words over in my head. "What?"

He shrugged, like it was oh so simple. "I'm not getting on that plane tomorrow."

CHAPTER TEN

WHERE SOME TRUTHS ARE SAID AND ARE AWFULLY HARD TO HEAR.

I'D JUST ROLLED my eyes and shook my head at him, completely disregarding what he'd said. "It's a nice thought," I'd told him, then stood there for a while not really knowin' what else I could say, and went to bed.

As always, after mustering was done, everyone had a few days off. Everyone was still there for breakfast though, even Travis. He was used to the crutch now and was getting around rather easily with it, but still not putting his foot on the floor.

Everyone was talking about what they were doing with their days off and who was heading into the Alice and when, and after they'd all gone and there was just me, George and Travis left at the table, George threw his serviette on his plate. "Well, Travis, your flight leaves at four. We'll need to be left here by eleven."

"I'm not going," he said.

George looked at me, then back to Travis. "What do you mean?"

"I mean, I'm not going," he repeated. "I told Charlie last night, but he thinks I'm joking." He turned in his seat and grabbed the crutch, slowly standing up. "Well, I'm not joking. I ain't going."

"Travis," I started. "You can't just stay."

"Says who?"

"Um, the Australian government," I said.

"So I'll fill in some more forms. Big deal." He slowly walked around the table, and George and I just watched him. "I told you, I'm staying."

I looked at George, and he blinked a few times before standing up and clapping me on the shoulder. "I'll leave this one up to you."

After a minute of blinking at the wall, I got up and followed Travis into my room. He was lying on my bed, his knee propped up on a pillow. "Travis, you can't just decide you're not going back."

"Well, I have."

"Why are you being so damn stubborn?"

"Because I have to be," he shot back at me. "Because you won't ask me to stay."

I heard the front door shut and realised our conversation could be heard. I shook my head and then answered calmly and quietly, "I'm not discussing this."

"Of course you're not," he said, rolling his eyes. Then he snapped. "And you think *I'm* stubborn?"

I clenched my jaw shut and looked out the window instead.

"Ma?" he called out. "Can you come here for a sec?"

I looked to the empty door, knowing Ma would be in it any second. "What are you doing?"

"I'm not getting on that plane."

"What do you mean you're not?" I asked. "Your ticket—"

"I don't care about the ticket."

"You have to go back."

He stared at me. "Is that what you want?"

"Travis, I…"

Ma stood in the doorway, looking between us. "Can you help me to the kitchen, please?" he asked, getting himself up. "I think I've overdone it. I did too much too soon," he said. "It's kinda hurting." He shuffled on his left foot and shoved the crutch under his right arm. I wanted to go to him, to help him, but my feet were rooted to the floor.

Ma was quick to prop herself under his left arm, helping him walk. "Sure, hon," she said. "But if your knee is sore, then maybe you should lie down."

"Not yet." He smiled at me as they walked past me to the door. "We *are* gonna discuss this. And apparently in this house, the kitchen is the place where things get said. And I got some things that need saying."

I stood in my room, blinking at where he'd just been. I had a fair idea what he was going to say. And I wanted him to say it. I wanted it so bad.

But I just… couldn't.

"Charlie!" Travis called out, presumably from the kitchen. "Can I speak to you please?"

I shook my head to myself. I half wanted to smile and half wanted to run.

I walked to the kitchen just as Ma was walking out. "Hear him out," she said. She looked sadder than I remember ever seeing her, but she patted my arm.

Travis was leaning against the table, the crutch under his arm, keeping his bandaged right leg bent off the floor. "This kitchen is neutral ground for conversation, yes?" he asked. He didn't wait for me to answer. "Because we're gonna talk."

"Travis…"

"God it's hot in here," he said, puffing his cheeks out when he breathed hard.

"We don't have to—" I started to say, but he cut me off.

"You know what? You can shut up and listen. After I'm done you can tell me if you don't want me to stay, but you can hear me out first."

I blinked at him. I don't think anyone had spoken to me like that.

"You're so hell-bent on being out here by yourself. You won't give anyone a chance. You think it's a special kind of hell on earth, but you love it anyway. And you know what? I get that. Because it's beautiful. But it doesn't have to be a life sentence, Charlie. You're so damn certain you'll be alone forever—*you're sure of it*—and it scares the hell outta you to think someone might wanna stay."

"I never said—"

"I said shut up and listen, I ain't done."

I think I heard a muffled laugh from outside, but I couldn't be sure.

"I want to stay. I want to be here. I want to work this farm with you. Lord fucking knows why, because you've done nothing but push me away, you've fought me over every possibility of there being an *us*, and why does it have to be so fucking hot!?" He threw up his hands and wiped the sweat from his brow. "It's a hundred and twenty damn degrees in this kitchen at seven in the morning!"

I opened my mouth to speak but he pointed his finger at me and my mouth snapped shut. Apparently he wasn't done talking.

"I don't know why, but something in my soul told me to come here." He shook his head. "I had a list of places to pick from but I *had* to come here. I just had to. Something in the back of my head, in my gut, told me to come here. Sutton

Station. The name stuck out at me, and right or wrong, I was coming here. And now I know why." He swallowed hard. "I knew after the first day. This godforsaken, red and unforgiving, hotter than fucking hell place was where I was supposed to be. With you."

I shook my head.

"Don't you dare say no," he said, shaking his head. "I'm standing here, telling you that I'm *in* this, and I know you want it. I *know* you want me to stay." He looked about ready to cry. "Fucking hell, Charlie," he whispered. "Don't tell me to go."

My heart was in my throat, squeezed tight. "Why? Why would you want this?"

The colour seemed to drain from his face. "I just told you why," he said quietly.

"I just don't understand why anyone would want this."

"Why? Because your mother didn't?" he asked. The question shocked me. "And you want to settle for a life of loneliness because that's what your father did? Is that what it is? Do you think you're not allowed to be happy, because he wasn't? Or because he told you you weren't allowed to be?" Travis was angry. He was standing on his good leg, balancing with the crutch, and he pointed his finger at me, the veins in his neck were strained and his blue eyes were fierce. "He told you no gay man could run this place and you fucking believe him."

I shook my head, but no words would come. I shook my head. "Travis..."

"Goddammit, Charlie," Travis said. "Don't just stand there like you don't know what to say."

"You wanna know?" I snapped. "You wanna know? This sand, *this red fucking dirt,* that's all there is. It'll burn ya feet, break your back and bleed you dry. And you know what? I fucking love it. It's part of me. It's who I am. It's *what* I am. And when my father dragged me, kicked me from here to Sydney to 'make a man outta me' I swore I would never come back. And now? Well, now I could never leave. This is all there is for me, and you know what? I've made my peace with that."

"Have you?"

"What? You think it doesn't bother me that I will have a solitary life? There's no *wife* for me, no partner, no one to grow old with me. How the fuck am I ever gonna meet someone, a *man* for that matter, when I live in the middle of the desert, hours from another living person? No man would sign up for this life. No *gay* man."

"See, that's where you're wrong."

I scoffed and threw my hands up. "And what makes you the expert? You've been here for three fucking weeks!"

He spun to look at me. He thumped his hand to his heart. "Because I would stay!"

I shook my head, dismissing his words. "You don't know what you're talking about."

Frustrated or angry or possibly both, he thumped his chest again. "Ask me!"

I opened my mouth and then closed it again. The words I wanted to say were stuck in my throat. "Ask you what?"

"Ask me to stay!" he cried, throwing his hands up. "It's not fucking difficult, Charlie. You open your damn mouth and you say 'I don't want you to go.' Tell me you don't know what it means, that this whole thing is confusing to you too, I don't care, just tell me that it will break your heart if I get on that plane. Try telling me that, Charlie." He ran his hands through his hair. "Tell me you'll buy some proper fucking coffee and ask me to stay."

He clenched his jaw and his eyes shone with tears. "I

thought you had demons, you know, like everyone else. But you're not fighting demons, Charlie," he said sadly. "You're fighting a ghost. And you don't even want to win."

"What do you want me to say?" I asked, probably louder than was necessary. "I grew up with that shit in my head, and I was resigned to bein' out here by myself. What the fuck else could I do? I had to keep this place going, it's in my blood, and if that meant never finding someone, then that's what I had to do!" I told him. "And then you came here, and..."

"And?"

"I don't know!" I cried, throwing my hands up. "You changed all that. Everything I thought I knew. You changed me."

He blew out a breath and started to smile.

"I don't know what it means," I told him. "I don't have a fucking clue what any of it means!"

"If you want me to go," he whispered. "If you really do, then tell me now."

I shook my head, reached out and grabbed his wrist. His eyes were so blue, so angry and hopeful. And as scared as I was, as much as I wanted to turn and run, I fucking stood there and let out a shaky breath.

And then from outside, before I could say anything else, the word "fag" cut through the quiet, followed by loud arguing. I'd never had a fight here yet and I wasn't about to start now.

I ran out of the kitchen, got to the front screen door, ready to stop whatever was just about to start.

I saw George first, standing in front of Fish. "I told you to shut your mouth," George said. I'd never heard him speak like that. Ever.

Fish threw his head back and laughed. It wasn't a happy

sound. "I saw those bites on him, but I didn't know who did 'em. Presumed it was Trudy, or even your missus, George, and now you's are telling me it's Travis? All this time, the boss has been a fucking queer."

George stepped forward and swung his right fist, knocking Fish off the veranda. I burst out through the door, and George spun to face me. He looked horrified and sorry, and his anger was now tinged with sadness.

Everyone was there. All my staff, and they stared at me. They knew I'm gay—they heard me talking to Travis, they saw the love bites—and they knew. There was no doubt.

This. *This* was what I wanted to avoid. All my life.

At all costs.

I turned on my heel to go back through the house, but Travis was in the doorway. I took a sideways step, and backing away from everyone, and I ran.

Just like I did when I was eighteen after I'd told my dad I was gay, and he told me I'd never be good enough. I ran then. And I ran now.

I ran to Shelby, and without time to saddle her, I grabbed her mane above the withers and hauled myself up onto her. I kicked her hard in the flanks, and she bolted, straight to the only place I wanted to go.

THE SCENERY WAS THE SAME. The red, red limestone ridge, the cluster of eucalypt trees and the clear blue water of the lagoon. It had been the same for tens of thousands of years.

Except now it was different.

He'd been here.

With me.

On the sheet of rock I sat on now, in the water. His laughter rang here. His hands had touched every inch of my skin here. He kissed me. I told him he was like no one else.

My head was a fucking mess.

He'd just told me he was falling in love with me. The most amazing gift, the biggest high. And then the ultimate low: my staff fighting over the one thing I'd tried to keep from them.

For the first time in god knows how long, I had hope. I felt something with Travis, and to have him want to stay with me filled me with something I couldn't quite name.

And then to have it stripped away, in the very next breath, almost made me wish I'd never known what it felt like to hope.

I could kick myself for wanting.

Out of the corner of my eye, I saw a man on a horse approaching. I recognised the way he sat in the saddle and, of course, the horse. I'd almost wished it was Travis, but in the end I was glad it wasn't.

The older guy got off his horse and walked over. "Got time for me, son?"

"Always, George," I answered. "Take a seat."

He sat down beside me, pulled off his boots, hiked up his jeans and put his feet in the water. He was quiet for a long while, and after a long slow breath, he said, "I understand if you have to let me go."

I shot him a look. "What?"

"For punchin' Fisher. I know you got no-fightin' rules."

"George," I said, shaking my head, disbelieving. "You're... you... I can't do this without you. You can't go," I stammered out.

"I punched a man," he started to say.

"You didn't just punch him," I said. "You knocked him clean off the porch."

George almost smiled. "He was saying some not nice stuff."

"I heard."

George sighed, and he looked... sad. "I kept telling him to mind his own business, but he wouldn't shut up. I won't tolerate no one talkin' 'bout you like that."

"It's okay," I said, my voice was just a whisper. Then I asked, "Have I got any staff left?"

"All of 'em. Except Fisher. I told him to pack his bags and be gone by the time I got back."

"How did you know where I was?"

He smiled that time. "You always come here to think, to get away." He looked up at the sky and sighed. "You did as a kid. You still do."

"You know me well."

He was quiet again, the way he usually was. Then he said, "We had a son. Did you know that?"

I shook my head. "No."

"His name was Joseph. He died when he was just a few days old," he said.

I could barely speak. "I didn't know."

He looked out across the landscape for a long while. I guessed his memories took him back to a place he didn't fancy going to often. Then out of the blue, he said, "Charlie, you're like a son to me and Ma." He kind of blurted it out, then shook his head, all kinds of embarrassed. "From the time you was born, when you rode your first pony, even when you were drivin' her mad, you were the light in Ma's eyes," George said.

"You and Ma mean the world to me."

Then his smile faded. "And there ain't nothing that you

could do or say that will change that," he said. "It kills me to hear you think you're not good enough. Charlie, you gotta get that voice outta your head. The one that tells you you're not good enough."

I looked out over the water and swallowed down the lump in my throat.

"My dad—"

"I know what he said to you. I was there. It was the only time I ever disagreed with your old man." He shook his head. "Charlie, you're a better man than he ever was."

I nodded and scrubbed the back of my hand at my stupid tears.

He gave me a minute, and then he said, "Can I ask you something?"

I nodded. "'Course."

"Now, you know it don't bother me none about who you fancy. It never has. Guess losing my own son taught me to appreciate rather than judge." George looked at me then. "But what about Travis?"

"What about him?"

"We didn't mean to be listenin' but you's was yellin' a bit," George said. "He doesn't want to go."

"Now, he doesn't. What about later?" I asked. "When he's sick of this place? The heat, the isolation, the dust? What then?"

"Not everyone's set on leavin' ya, Charlie."

I looked out across the horizon, not wanting to argue the point.

He was quiet for a while. "That night you were looking for Travis, yellin' his name," he said, talking softly. "We heard you callin' for him. Broke Ma's heart every time you yelled his name." He gave me a sad smile. "It got quieter the farther you went out, but it was the hardest thing I've ever had to listen to."

I looked at him and instead of being able to speak, more tears fell down my face.

"Charlie, how does he make you feel?"

I scrubbed at my face and wiped my nose on the back of my hand. "What?"

George smiled. "I'll tell you something, and I don't want you to go repeatin' it to no one. But she makes me honest. I try harder because of that woman of mine, and I think if I can go to sleep each night knowin' I did my best for her that day, then I did alright."

I smiled at him and my eyes welled with tears again. That was the closest thing to poetry I'd ever heard. They had a relationship, a partnership, spanning decades and I wanted that. With every cell in my body, I wanted to know what it felt like to love and to be loved like that.

"I want that," I said, barely getting the words out through my tears. "Why can't I have someone to love me like that?"

George's face crumpled. "Charlie, son... you do." He took a deep, shaky breath. "He's back at the house, cursing your stubborn hide."

I stared at him, not really sure how to answer. "Oh."

"He's a good man."

I nodded.

"Do you want him to stay?"

I swallowed again and let out a shaky breath. "More than anything." It felt good to say that out loud, to admit it, was like a weight came off my shoulders. "Peace," I finally admitted. "He makes me feel at peace. And happy. And scared shitless."

George smiled at me. "Sounds like love to me."

My eyes opened wide and I shook my head, but George just laughed. "I don't care about what's gone on between you," he said. "Ain't nobody's business but yours. But he's right about one thing." I looked at him then, waiting for him to continue. "Ghosts ain't no company for the living, Charlie," he said quietly. "You need to let your father go."

I didn't say anything to that. I guess my tears said it all.

"And he's right about something else."

I wiped my face. "Yeah, what's that?"

"You need to go tell that boy to stay."

CHAPTER ELEVEN

WHOEVER SANG ABOUT SORRY BEIN' THE HARDEST WORD OBVIOUSLY NEVER HAD TO SAY GOODBYE.

THE RIDE HOME was slow and steady. George was beside me, letting me have my peace and quiet, but in a *you're-not-really-alone* kind of way. I was in knots about facing Travis, excited and petrified in equal measure. Like I wanted to run to see him, but my body was too scared to move. As we neared the house, I broke the silence.

"Do you think he's still there?" I asked, wiping the sweat from my forehead. "What if he left with the others? What if he thought fuck this shit and left?"

George did a mix of head-shaking and smiling. "He's as stubborn as you. If he said he weren't leavin' then he's not going anywhere."

"But what if he—"

"Then you haul your arse into Alice and stop him."

I breathed out loudly and nodded. "And Fish is gone?"

"And told never to come back," George added. "I told him you'd sort out what he's owed, and if he muttered one more word about Ma or you, I'd pull his head from his neck."

I snorted out a laugh, then sighed. "Thank you. And

sorry. I'm sorry you had to do that, but I'm grateful that you did."

George gave me a smile and we rode our horses to the fence in the cooler shade near the shed. I climbed off Shelby and let the reins slip over her head. George took them off me. "You can't put it off. He would've seen us come in. He knows you're out here."

"I don't know what to say to him."

"I ain't no expert," George said, "and God knows I've made mistakes that shoulda cost me more than they did, but I can tell ya the best place to start is with the truth."

And if I didn't need any more encouragement, Shelby nudged me toward the house. The first few steps were the hardest. But then halfway across the yard, I kinda had to see him, and by the time I got to the veranda steps, I took them two at a time and called his name as I all but ran into the house. "Travis!"

I looked right, into the lounge room, but he wasn't there. So I ducked into the hall and checked my room. "Travis!" Then I checked his room, but still couldn't find him. And it dawned on me, that maybe, just maybe, he'd gone.

"Travis?" I called out as I made my way back into the foyer. He wasn't in my office or the dining room. I all but ran into the kitchen. "Trav—"

And there he was. Sitting at the table with the crutch at his side, eating a sandwich like it was just any old day, talking to Ma.

They both stopped and stared at me. "Travis," I said, out of breath. "I thought you'd gone."

"I told you I wasn't going."

I grinned at him, and Ma stood up like she was about to leave, and smiled at me. "I was just telling Travis the story of when you rode your first bull," she said. "You were six."

"It wasn't a very big one," I said, not taking my eyes off Travis.

"It scared me half to death," Ma said as she walked around the table to me. "And about a hundred things you've done since then. You'd think I'd be used to it by now."

"Ma," I said, finally looking at her and fighting new tears. With everything George had told me still fresh in my head, I quickly scooped her up in a hug. "I got real lucky when you and George walked onto this farm. I couldn't have picked a better mum than you."

I let her go, and she put her hand to her mouth. Her eyes filled with tears. "Oh, love," she said, her voice all croaky. She put one hand to my face.

"I should have told you that before now."

Ma smiled as the tears rolled down her cheeks. She looked over to Travis. "Here, look at me, taking up all your time," she said, shaking her head. "You two have so much to talk about. Where's my Joseph Brown?" she asked, but more to herself, because she was already walking into the foyer.

I looked at Travis then, knowing this was it.

"I'm sorry I ran," I said. I swallowed hard. "It's not easy for me to talk about things, and you just blurt them all out like it's no big deal. I can't do that. Well, I mean, I'll have to learn how to do that."

Travis smiled, and taking his crutch, he stood up and slowly walked over to me. "You just managed with Ma okay."

"That took me twenty years to say that."

Travis chuckled and stood in front of me. "Will it take that long with me?"

I shook my head. "No." I put my hand to his face and ran the pad of my thumb along his cheek. "I have something really important to tell you," I said.

"What's that?" he asked quietly, still smiling.

I stared into his eyes so he would see the sincerity. I swallowed hard—my mouth was suddenly dry. "Stay."

Travis grinned. "You're a bit late."

I nodded. "I know. But I should have said it before. I want you to know that I want you here. More than anything." Then I said it again. "Stay," I said, louder this time. "You're right. I don't know what this means, and I don't know how long it will be before this land drives you away from me, but I don't want you to get on that plane."

Travis smiled at my tirade. "You found some words."

I just kept going. "I want you to stay. With me. Here, in the middle of fucking nowhere, but I think if you gave it a chance, you'd learn to love it too."

He was grinning now. "I already do love it here. I wouldn't stay if I didn't," he said softly. He cupped one hand to my face and ran his thumb across my bottom lip. "But I'm not staying because of the farm, Charlie. I'm staying for you."

"You really are, aren't you?"

He nodded and leaned in as if to kiss me. His face was so close to mine. "Well, you did ask."

I laughed, relieved, and he pulled my face to his, pressing his lips to mine. "You're a stubborn man."

"You know," he said. "Me being stubborn saved George a trip to Alice and you a trip to the airport."

"How so?"

"Well, George would have had to have driven me to town, then you would have stayed here and been all impossible, and Ma would have yelled at you for a being an arse and then you would have taken the chopper to the airport to stop my plane. It would have been all romantic and shit but expensive all round and completely unnecessary."

I was smiling at him. "Is that so?"

"All you had to do was ask me to stay."

"Stay."

"You already asked me." He let the crutch fall to the ground and hopped on his one foot. He grabbed my face and pulled me in for a kiss. And in a moment of rare vulnerability, he whispered, "Don't make me regret it."

I swallowed hard. "I don't know what I'm doing. And I don't know if any of my staff will be back in two days or not. If they won't work for me because they know I'm gay, or if they'll be okay with this, I mean, Fish is already gone, so I'm one man down—"

"No you're not," he said. "You got me. I can't do much with my knee just yet, but it won't take too long."

I tried to smile but needed to warn him. "Travis, I really don't know what I'm doing... with this whole relationship thing, so you'll need to tell me if I need telling."

Travis smiled and pecked my lips. "I will."

I put my forehead to his and whispered against his mouth. "Thank you. For telling me what I needed to hear."

He pulled back a little and said, "You're welcome. I just saved you the hassle of figuring it out before it was too late."

I laughed quietly. "I would have let you go and been miserable forever."

He shook his head. "Oh. One more thing," he said. "I've also saved you the hassle of asking me to move my stuff into your room."

I laughed, louder this time, and pulled his face to mine for a kiss. Then I stared into his eyes, those blue eyes along with that disarming smile that I found sitting in my kitchen just four weeks ago. "Are we really doing this?"

He smiled. "We really are."

TWO WEEKS LATER
GHOSTS AND GOODBYES, AND FINALLY BEIN'
FREE.

EVERYTHING at the station had returned to normal. Well, as normal as it was going to get, given that Travis was now a permanent employee. And he was also my live-in boyfriend —a fact that still surprised me, squeezed my heart just a little every time I thought of it.

Everyone came back to work after the weekend in the Alice. Everyone except Fish, not that he was welcome. No one cared that me and Travis were together. They knew there'd be no favouritism or leniency on my behalf when it came to him. I was a hard boss, but they also knew Travis was a hard worker.

While he was laid up with his sore knee, he did what he could around the house and yard. We spoke to his mum on Skype a few times; she was understandably upset that Travis wasn't coming home, but she wasn't surprised. He promised he'd be home to see her again at some point and even said I'd tag along with him. He filled out more government forms to extend his stay, and Ma simply adored him.

Or she adored how happy he made me.

Everything was pretty damn good. But there was something I still needed to do.

After dinner, when the storms were blowing in and the skies were an angry palette of purple and grey, Travis and I rode a dirt bike to just a few hundred metres from the house. The winds were picking up, adding red sand swirls to the mix. I turned the key to the off position and the engine cut, leaving nothing but the sound of the wind and silence.

I was nervous about doing this, even though it was my idea. I *needed* to do this. Travis's leg was getting better—still nowhere near fully healed, but he was well enough to climb onto the back of a bike with me. He got off first, still favouring his sore leg. I swung my leg over the bike and kicked the stand down.

When I turned around, Travis asked me if I was okay.

I gave him a small smile. "I am."

"Are you ready to do this?"

I nodded this time, and with him by my side, I walked over to my father's grave. I hadn't been back since the day we buried him. I never had anything to say.

Until now.

I stared at the headstone for a long while, then with a deep breath, I took the first step in letting go.

"Dad, I want to introduce you to someone," I said, looking to the man beside me. "His name is Travis Craig. And he's wonderful, Dad."

Travis smiled at me. He never spoke, just listened. He was there just because I needed him to be.

"He's funny, kind, smarter than anyone I know. He makes me happy, Dad. Happier than I ever thought possible." I exhaled loudly. "I'm not here telling you this for your approval, because God knows I'd never get it. I'm here telling you this because I'm not hiding anymore."

It felt so good to say that. As stupid as it was to say it to a slab of marble, to thin air, it didn't matter. I was saying this to my father, and it felt so fucking good. The emotions burst in my chest and formed as tears in my eyes.

"I'm not scared of you anymore," I said. My voice cracked, and Travis put his arm around me. "I'm not scared of you anymore."

I took a deep breath and blinked back tears.

"I've got some news for you, Dad," I said. "Even though you swore it would never happen, *could* never happen, Sutton Station is run by a fairy. That's right, a fucking queer, faggot. And you know what? I'm doing a damn good job."

Travis rubbed reassuring circles on my back. He knew I'd just repeated my father's hurtful words back to him. He knew how much those very words had haunted me.

"I will run this place better than you ever could," I told my father. "And I'll do it with a man in my bed." I shook my head, took a deep breath and exhaled loudly. The storm brewed above us, thunder rumbled and lightning pierced the clouds.

"I love him, Dad."

Travis's hand stilled on my back, his breath hitched and I could feel his eyes on me. "Charlie..."

I turned to him. "It's true. I do," I told him. "And he should know. My father should know. It's real, and you're the best thing to ever happen to me. He told me I would never be happy, that I didn't deserve it." I let my tears fall. "But I *am* happy. And I *do* deserve it."

Travis nodded and pulled me against him, letting me cry into his neck. "I love you, too," he whispered in my ear and kissed the side of my head. He held me tighter and only let go when I pulled back.

He kept one arm around me, and when I was done talking to my father, he stayed with me at the motorbike for a while. He leaned against the seat and wrapped his arms around me, just letting there be silence. Letting me say goodbye to ghosts in my head.

"I'm ready to go back now," I told him.

"Are you sure?"

I nodded and drove us back to the house. Only when we walked inside this time, I stopped inside the door.

As always, Travis put his hat on the hallstand. "You okay?" he asked quietly.

I nodded but picked up his hat. I took mine off, and looking them both over, I put his hat on the centre hook. The hook that had been mine forever was now his.

Then I put my hat on the hook closest to the door. My father's hook. Only it wasn't his anymore. It was mine. His ghost didn't live here anymore.

I looked at Travis. His eyes were wide and warm. I think he was waiting for more tears, but this time I smiled.

The skies outside rumbled and roared, and thunder ripped through the silence. Travis slid his hand around my neck and pulled me in for a hard kiss as the first of the rains fell.

The rain, this man washed away the demons—the ghosts, as he called them—and set me free.

ABOUT THE AUTHOR

N.R. Walker is an Australian author, who loves her genre of gay romance. She loves writing and spends far too much time doing it, but wouldn't have it any other way.

She is many things: a mother, a wife, a sister, a writer. She has pretty, pretty boys who live in her head, who don't let her sleep at night unless she gives them life with words.

She likes it when they do dirty, dirty things... but likes it even more when they fall in love. She used to think having people in her head talking to her was weird, until one day she happened across other writers who told her it was normal.

She's been writing ever since...

---

nrwalker.net

Exchange of Hearts

The Spencer Cohen Series, Book One

The Spencer Cohen Series, Book Two

The Spencer Cohen Series, Book Three

The Spencer Cohen Series, Yanni's Story

Blood & Milk

The Weight Of It All

A Very Henry Christmas (The Weight of It All 1.5)

Perfect Catch

Switched

Imago

Imagines

Imagoes

Red Dirt Heart Imago

On Davis Row

Finders Keepers

Evolved

Galaxies and Oceans

Private Charter

Nova Praetorian

A Soldier's Wish

Upside Down

The Hate You Drink

Sir

Tallowwood

Reindeer Games

The Dichotomy of Angels

Throwing Hearts

Pieces of You - Missing Pieces #1

Pieces of Me - Missing Pieces #2

Pieces of Us - Missing Pieces #3

Lacuna

Tic-Tac-Mistletoe

Bossy

Code Red

Dearest Milton James

Dearest Malachi Keogh

Christmas Wish List

Code Blue

Davo

The Kite

Learning Curve

Merry Christmas Cupid

To the Moon and Back

Second Chance at First Love

Outrun the Rain

Into the Tempest

Touch the Lightning

EWB - Enemies With Benefits

Holiday Heart Strings

Bloom

The Men from Echo Creek

Titles in Audio:

Cronin's Key

Cronin's Key II

Cronin's Key III

Red Dirt Heart

Red Dirt Heart 2

Red Dirt Heart 3

Red Dirt Heart 4

The Weight Of It All

Switched

Point of No Return

Breaking Point

Starting Point

Spencer Cohen Book One

Spencer Cohen Book Two

Spencer Cohen Book Three

Yanni's Story

On Davis Row

Evolved

Elements of Retrofit

Clarity of Lines

Sense of Place

Blind Faith

Through These Eyes

Blindside

Finders Keepers

Galaxies and Oceans

Nova Praetorian

Upside Down

Sir

Tallowwood

Imago

Throwing Hearts

Sixty Five Hours

Taxes and TARDIS

The Dichotomy of Angels

The Hate You Drink

Pieces of You

Pieces of Me

Pieces of Us

Tic-Tac-Mistletoe

Lacuna

Bossy

Code Red

Learning to Feel

Dearest Milton James

Dearest Malachi Keogh

Three's Company

Christmas Wish List

Code Blue

Davo

The Kite

Learning Curve

Merry Christmas Cupid

To the Moon and Back

Second Chance at First Love

Outrun the Rain

Into the Tempest

Touch the Lightning

EWB

Holiday Heart Strings

Bloom

Series Collections:

Red Dirt Heart Series

Turning Point Series

Thomas Elkin Series

Spencer Cohen Series

Imago Series

Blind Faith Series

Missing Pieces Series

The Storm Boys Series

Free Reads:

Sixty Five Hours

Learning to Feel

His Grandfather's Watch (And The Story of Billy and Hale)

The Twelfth of Never (Blind Faith 3.5)

Twelve Days of Christmas (Sixty Five Hours Christmas)

Best of Both Worlds

Translated Titles:

Italian

Fiducia Cieca (Blind Faith)

Attraverso Questi Occhi (Through These Eyes)

Preso alla Sprovvista (Blindside)

Il giorno del Mai (Blind Faith 3.5)

Cuore di Terra Rossa Serie (Red Dirt Heart Series)

Natale di terra rossa (Red dirt Christmas)

Intervento di Retrofit (Elements of Retrofit)

A Chiare Linee (Clarity of Lines)

Senso D'appartenenza (Sense of Place)

Spencer Cohen Serie (including Yanni's Story)

Punto di non Ritorno (Point of No Return)

Punto di Rottura (Breaking Point)

Punto di Partenza (Starting Point)

Imago (Imago)

Imagines

Il desiderio di un soldato (A Soldier's Wish)

Scambiato (Switched)

Tallowwood

The Hate You Drink

Ho trovato te (Finders Keepers)

Cuori d'argilla (Throwing Hearts)

Galassie e Oceani (Galaxies and Oceans)

Il peso di tut (The Weight of it All)

Pieces of You - Missing Pieces 1

French

Confiance Aveugle (Blind Faith)

A travers ces yeux: Confiance Aveugle 2 (Through These Eyes)

Aveugle: Confiance Aveugle 3 (Blindside)

À Jamais (Blind Faith 3.5)

Cronin's Key Series

Au Coeur de Sutton Station (Red Dirt Heart)

Partir ou rester (Red Dirt Heart 2)

Faire Face (Red Dirt Heart 3)

Trouver sa Place (Red Dirt Heart 4)

Le Poids de Sentiments (The Weight of It All)

Un Noël à la sauce Henry (A Very Henry Christmas)

Une vie à Refaire (Switched)

Evolution (Evolved)

Galaxies & Océans

Qui Trouve, Garde (Finders Keepers)

Sens Dessus Dessous (Upside Down)

La Haine au Fond du Verre (The hate You Drink)

Tallowwood

Spencer Cohen Series

Thomas Elkin One

Lacuna

German

Flammende Erde (Red Dirt Heart)

Lodernde Erde (Red Dirt Heart 2)

Sengende Erde (Red Dirt Heart 3)

Ungezähmte Erde (Red Dirt Heart 4)

Vier Pfoten und ein bisschen Zufall (Finders Keepers)

Ein Kleines bisschen Versuchung (The Weight of It All)

Ein Kleines Bisschen Fur Immer (A Very Henry Christmas)

Weil Leibe uns immer Bliebt (Switched)

Drei Herzen eine Leibe (Three's Company)

Über uns die Sterne, zwischen uns die Liebe (Galaxies and Oceans)

Unnahbares Herz (Blind Faith 1)

Sehendes Herz (Blind Faith 2)

Hoffnungsvolles Herz (Blind Faith 3)

Verträumtes Herz (Blind Faith 3.5)

Thomas Elkin: Verlangen in neuem Design

Thomas Elkin: Leidenschaft in klaren

Thomas Elkin: Vertrauen in bester Lage

Traummann töpfern leicht gemacht (Throwing Hearts)

Sir

So Unendlich Viel Liebe (To the Moon and Back)

Thai

Sixty Five Hours (Thai translation)

Finders Keepers (Thai translation)

Spanish

Sesenta y Cinco Horas (Sixty Five Hours)

Los Doce Días de Navidad

Código Rojo (Code Red)

Código Azul (Code Blue)

Queridísimo Milton James

Queridísimo Malachi Keogh

El Peso de Todo (The Weight of it All)

Tres Muérdagos en Raya: Serie Navidad en Hartbridge

Lista De Deseos Navideños: Serie Navidad en Hartbridge

Feliz Navidad Cupido: Serie Navidad en Hartbridge

Spencer Cohen Libro Uno

Spencer Cohen Libro Dos

Spencer Cohen Libro Tres

Davo

Hasta la Luna y de Vuelta

Venciendo A La Lluvia

En la Tempestad

El Toque del Rayo

Corazón De Tierra Roja

Corazón De Tierra Roja 2

Corazón De Tierra Roja 3

Corazón De Tierra Roja 4

ECB (Enemigos con Beneficios)

Floral

Chinese

Blind Faith

Japanese

Bossy

Portuguese

Sessenta e Cinco Horas